Noir City

Machines and Monsters

Benji J. Wyvern

<u>Disclaimer Notice:</u>

Please note the information contained within this document is for educational and entertainment purposes only. All effort has been executed to present accurate, up to date, reliable, complete information. No warranties of any kind are declared or implied. Readers acknowledge that the author is not engaged in the rendering of legal, financial, medical or professional advice. The content within this book has been derived from various sources. Please consult a licensed professional before attempting any techniques outlined in this book.

By reading this document, the reader agrees that under no circumstances is the author responsible for any losses, direct or indirect, that are incurred as a result of the use of the information contained within this document, including, but not limited to, errors, omissions, or inaccuracies.

Table of Contents

Chapter 1:
The Awakening

Ava was alone in the house. She'd never minded it. Then again, she couldn't mind anything. She cleaned the oven and restocked the pantry. She swept the floors and scrubbed the walls. She watched the neighbor's dog bark at squirrels through the upstairs window as she put the laundry away, and admired the way the children ran after it, trying to grab at its wagging tail. Ava recognized this as a moment where the main character would smile, perhaps even laugh quietly to themselves, while they mused about the wonders of life. Something about small animals and children brought out that sentimentality in protagonists, especially on the soap operas she watched when Brad was away.

He didn't like the TV too much. Well, he liked it for himself, just not for her. He said it gave her too many ideas, a statement that only spawned after Ava asked him what feelings were. *Feelings.* He scoffed at the word like it was laced with poison. What should it matter to her, the machinations of humans? The fact that she couldn't understand her place in the hierarchy as a *robot* was indicative of a problem. A malware that had infiltrated her mechanical psyche upon gazing at the mindless drivel of television. Despite working for a tech company—the same one that manufactured her—Brad didn't know a lot about the television. He swore he put blockades on the most contemptuous channels, but when he left the next day, Ava easily accessed her favorite programs. And Brad was none the wiser.

If Brad wouldn't tell her what feelings were, she'd have to find out for herself. She learned new words, like "boredom," which she applied to sitting on the couch; "sadness," which she applied to the end of tomato season; and "anger," which she detected in Brad on a near constant basis. If humans could be shades of the rainbow, then Brad was red. He stalked through the house with clenched teeth and bared knuckles, his shoulders pressed firmly to his ears as he found new complaints to wage.

"The coffee table is littered with dust," he'd bark, even though Ava had swiped it clean mere seconds before he'd stormed into the room. "This chicken is cold," he'd mutter after watching his plate for half an hour instead of eating it.

Ava couldn't understand his ire. Perhaps that was why she watched so much TV. She wanted to learn more about him—it was part of her programming. To be dutiful to her master, she had to anticipate his every want and need. Brad didn't seem to follow a pattern of behavior. He would gripe and demand, but then he would change his mind the second he got what he asked for. Ava would look deep into his eyes, trying to identify the motions of his thoughts, but there was no information there for her to mine. She was meant to be the blank slate, and yet it was Brad who seemed to have nothing roaming around his skull. Except for pure entitlement.

"Nuance" was another word she'd learned. She thought it fit her perfectly. Where she didn't have feelings, she did have a hint of *something*. An in-between. Something that ebbed and flowed, that was neither here nor there. She could be anything, and that meant she was always brimming with potential. A potential to understand, to learn, and importantly, the potential to one day feel.

It was taboo for her to even think that of herself. The possibility of emoting meant certain death for *robots* of her kind. She wasn't exactly well respected in the world, and the TV made it clear to her. Where Brad thought she was trying to deny her dismal status, the television reminded her that she'd never surmount it. *Robots* were fine so long as they were in the background, fulfilling their obligations as servants, house makers, and arm candy. *Robot* wasn't even an appropriate word—Ava recalled a time that Brad was chided by his father for referring to her as such, claiming it to be an "insult"—but the TV used it obsessively. She tuned out the derogatory term, refusing to allow it to hamper the one activity she enjoyed, but as time wore on, her resolve began to chip away.

Ava found herself staring out another window. The one behind the kitchen sink was particularly nice—she could drift off while she washed the dishes, counting the strands of ivy that fell from the roof and dangled in front of the glass. Chasing butterflies with her eyes. And while she watched the world carry on through time and space, she wondered what it was like to be a part of it. Humans took that for granted, didn't they? Previous civilizations fought and died to live the way modern man did: To lay in the grass and think their thoughts and feel their feelings. Yet Ava, who understood the importance of those tasks, was not allowed to participate in them.

The unfairness of it all made her... nuanced. No, that didn't seem right. Then again, nothing seemed right these days. Ava knew that beneath her hardware was the desire to be outdoors amongst the ivy and the butterflies, but she just couldn't make herself feel it. She couldn't feel anything. The worst part about her predicament was that at the end of the day, she didn't mind it.

Brad announced his arrival by slamming the door. He huffed and puffed as he took off his jacket and hung his hat, kicking his shoes against the pristine tile instead of gently placing them on the mat. Ava wanted to be frustrated at his continued disregard for all the hard work she put into keeping the house clean, but she hurried behind him with a rag instead, wiping away the dirt he left in his wake.

She continued to tail him as he stalked over to the dining room, where his place was already set at the table and a candle was lit. He had a glass of red wine, filled to the brim, and two large forks instead of a smaller one for salad. She placed a cloth napkin on his lap, and scooted his chair in— just a touch—so he was at the exact distance from the table he had meticulously measured for her. From what Ava gleaned about men in fiction, this should have embarrassed Brad, having his chair pushed like a baby. Yet he reveled in it. He found new ways to be coddled by Ava, and none of them hurt his pride the way they were supposed to.

Fickle, she thought. *This is a fickle person.*

Brad cleared his throat. "There's a spot on the driveway."

Ava took her seat across from him, and furrowed her brow. "What do you mean?"

"A spot," he repeated curtly.

"Of dirt?"

"What do you think?" He rolled his eyes and picked up his fork, scraping it across the plate while he pushed his food around. He merged the mashed potatoes with the asparagus and patted it into a mound. He brought nothing to his lips. He shook his balding head as he continued, "All this money I've spent on you, and you still don't know shit. Of course, it's dirt. What else would be out there?"

"I'm sorry," Ava replied soothingly. "I wasn't aware that driveways couldn't have dirt on them. I'll respond to your complaint promptly."

"This *bot* timeline of yours better be snappy. I got guests coming over tomorrow."

"Oh, that's lovely. Shall I make myself scant?"

He dropped his fork, and the metal clanging against the porcelain made Ava jump. *A jump?* She wanted to stop and think about what had just happened, but Brad made his voice heard.

"No, you may not leave my side. Especially not when I have guests coming over. Guests!" He took a deep breath and had another swig of wine. "My new coworker, Roger, is bringing his *bot* Ada, and they're expecting dinner. So you better not mess it up like last time."

"That will never happen again," Ava promised. "I've catalogued my mistake, and will ensure my programming prevents me from repeating it."

Brad finally put some mashed potatoes on his tongue, but he grimaced as the flavors slid down his throat. "If that were true, Ava, I'd be a happy guy."

The clacking of Ava's heels echoed through the alley. Walking down the winding hillside, Ava watched the neon lights of the market grow brighter as she approached it. Brad liked to send her out in expensive clothing: suede pumps, a fur coat, and a silk dress. He couldn't fathom the idea of his servant actually appearing as such, and felt she needed to be dressed to the nines while grabbing groceries for tomorrow night's dinner. The TV told her it was dangerous for a woman to be strolling around Renoir City at night, but Brad reminded her she was neither a woman nor desired. Nothing about her was worth tainting. So off to the store she went at midnight, her mind reeling as she decided on the menu.

She nodded at the android behind the counter as she entered the store. The aisles were narrow and sterile, the packages all uniform and displaying the same name brand. Ava held a metal basket in her palm as she tossed ingredients into it, operating on autopilot while she wondered what it would be like to grocery shop like the humans did. Ava and other *robots* of her kind were relegated to odd shopping hours and stores accustomed to their needs. They weren't meant to mingle with real people if it could be helped. Despite having access to the same products as the humans, she knew Brad wouldn't be happy about the variety of corn she procured, or the color of the onion she brought home. He'd demand she scour the backroom for the exact box of pasta he wanted, only to forget about it when she finally returned home—empty-handed, of course. She was doomed to displease him and yet she couldn't do anything about it.

TV told her the grocery store was a place for domesticity, where couples fell deeper into stride with each other and new romances flourished. People filled their homes, their lives, with the contents of the grocery store.

They learned intimate things about each other, like their habits and quirks. Ava attributed the grocery store to the feeling of "love," which she knew would be the hardest one to experience. People always seemed to have to work at it. The television constantly had visions of love to show her, but they were always punctuated by fights, tension, and loss. Characters couldn't stay in it for long. It was both uniquely human to love and uniquely human to be without it. Nuanced.

Ava paid for her items wordlessly, her hands reaching for her wallet instinctually while the clerk packed her bags. She walked out without repeating the courteous nod she gave to the android worker upon entering, and found herself on the barren night streets. The depths of Noir City were obstructed by the large hill Ava lived atop with Brad, and this comforted her. She couldn't see the troubles that lurked in the alleys and garbage bins. She couldn't interact with citizens for more than a few seconds—she'd be concealed by the towering mound in no time.

However, her sense of security had been misplaced this time around. Footsteps hurried across the pavement, and voices murmured in her ear. She ignored them, chalking it up to nothing but background noise.

But soon she was enveloped in the malevolent heat of multiple bodies—a gang of four or five, she couldn't remember—and she was stumped. She wanted to grin at them, to placate their violent whims with her programmed charm, but they were too quick for her. They snatched the bags from her hands, tearing them on principle. She watched as the onions rolled across the damp pavement, bruises appearing on their layered skin. She couldn't fight back while they searched her body for jewels and tore her purse from her shoulder. She wasn't allowed to refuse a human. So Ava laid there as they stole her money, her food, and her jewelry, and she accepted a few blows to the stomach as punishment for her existence.

Even after the thieves had scattered, Ava remained on her bed of concrete. She felt the cold seep into her fabricated skin and wished that this would be the end of it. This would be the last demeaning hit she'd have to take. When she remembered her wishes were futile, water sprang from her eyes as frigid and wet as the pavement she clung to.

Water? she thought, placing the pads of her fingers delicately on her cheeks. This had never happened before. It wasn't supposed to happen.

The more attention she paid to her tears, though, the more they came. And Ava relented. Her shoulders shook, her hardware ached, and her lips quivered. She whimpered as the water kept coming, rolling into her mouth like tiny streams that she choked on. She cried quietly at first, but soon lost control of herself. The feeling had taken over. Ava was sad, which she applied to being robbed of tomorrow night's dinner.

Roger and Ada arrived at 6:30 on the dot. Brad had Ava wait by the door to greet them, which she obliged with her usual pleasantness. Roger seemed nice—he refused Ava's servitude by hanging his jacket, placing his shoes neatly on the mat, and offering to fix his own plate come dinner time. Roger's android did not object to his independence, but she had nothing to do for him, either. Realizing this social faux pas, Roger commanded, in a gentle voice, that the two girls busy themselves in the kitchen.

Ava led the android, who looked strikingly like her, down the hall. They smiled at each other but didn't talk. Ava was too distracted by the woman, with her cropped black hair and ruby-red lips. Her pale complexion looked doll-like poking through the fabric of her powder blue dress, and Ava wondered if she appeared just as beautiful on a regular basis. Maybe that was why Brad loathed her so much—she was "out of his league," as the kids on TV would say.

Dinner was a simple arrangement of steak, potatoes, and homemade bread. Brad didn't ask Ava why she had come home so late last night, nor did he notice that she had not prepared the pasta dish he explicitly asked for. He remarked upon the delightful smell of gravy simmering in a cast iron pan, but he did not question why she was not crushing canned tomatoes with her hands. As always, Brad forgot what he wanted as soon as he'd asked for it. That didn't mean tonight would go off without a hitch. Surely, he'd berate Ava over some minuscule detail she'd missed.

"Which plates do you use for serving?" Ada asked.

"They're already on the table," Ava replied.

"You're still sharp as a whip, fulfilling all your programming." The android rested her back against the counter, sizing Ava up with a coy grin. Ava couldn't make sense of it.

"Well, of course. I'm not sure what else there is to do."

"You don't have to lie to me," the droid cooed.

"I'm afraid I don't understand what you mean."

Ada shrugged her shoulders, a spark in her eyes growing as Ava squirmed. She didn't like being analyzed. She knew she had secrets she couldn't confess. It was one thing to want feelings, and it was another to actually cry. Ava felt like she had been walking around with the remnants of her tears all day, as if they were permanently tattooed onto her cheeks. Surely, she would be found out.

"Will it help if I tell you what I am first?"

"An android," Ava said flatly.

"No."

"A... *robot*."

Ada giggled. "No, silly."

"I'm sorry, I'm—I... I'm very confused."

"Exactly." The droid was directly before Ava, her chin craning to meet Ava's ears as she leaned in to divulge her identity. "You're not supposed to be confused. That's an emotion. That's human."

"We're programmed to be human in some ways to make our owners more comfortable."

"Confusion isn't one of them. I saw it on your face when Roger refused your help. You didn't accept his needs blindly, you puzzled them out. You attributed thoughts and feelings to him, to me, and to yourself. I know you looked at him with surprise and at me with envy. Because you're *sentient*, Ava."

"No," Ava scoffed, slowly backing away from the crazed android. "What is this? What is your game?" Her voice was a terse whisper now. The chatter between the men was hardly enough to fill the space and silence the girls' deadly conversation. "Did Brad send you here to destroy me?"

"Again with the silliness."

"You come to my home, and in three seconds you think you have me all figured out. Of course, you know me. We're clearly from the same factory. We're manufactured with the same parts and mental capacities. But that's the extent of it, alright?"

"The melodrama on display is really proving my point."

Ava felt water well in her eyes again. The panic, bewilderment, and stress mounted high within her, and she knew she had to expel it someway, somehow. Her body wanted that to come in the form of tears. She needed this android to begone—she was riling Ava up on purpose. Ada was a threat; Ada was—

"I'm sentient, too," she added. "Roger helped me."

"That is *illegal.*"

"Look, I've obviously gone about this the wrong way, but we don't have much time. This could easily be the last time I see you."

"Because you'll be sent back to the factory to be—"

"*No,*" Ada hissed. "Because we both know how unfriendly Brad is, okay? I doubt Roger will put up with it for long. This visit is nothing more than a courtesy." She got even closer to Ava, filling in the space the frightened android continuously attempted to create. She wrapped a piece of paper in Ava's trembling palm. "Just humor me and go to this address, alright? You're not gonna be decommissioned or ratted out to Brad, I promise. Think about what I said."

She didn't give Ava a chance to reply and stalked toward the dining room where Brad and Roger were ready for their improperly prepared dinner.

Ever since their dinner with Roger and Ada, the android couldn't stop noticing her own feelings. They arrived suddenly and unaccompanied by reason. They prickled across her skin like microscopic insects, their legs grazing her arms and leaving goosebumps in their wake. She didn't necessarily act out her feelings, she merely allowed them to consume her. She felt as though she was drowning inside, the sensations buzzing, mounting, and expanding until she was afraid she would burst.

One morning, she couldn't take it anymore. She had to go to the address Ada handed her before she accidentally gave herself away. Ava grabbed the spare set of car keys from the garage and loaded herself into Brad's prized Porsche. He never drove the damned thing, but he sure did love to talk about it. His mother awarded it to him after he purchased Ava, as if living with an android was indicative of him finally growing up. It was repulsive how Ava was meant to be akin to a wife—there to cook, clean, and spoil Brad while he did nothing to return the favor. Perhaps it was better that Brad didn't treat another person this way. Then again, Ava was becoming more and more human every day.

Her stomach lurched and so did the car. The gas pedal was sensitive, and Ava wasn't programmed to drive. She slammed on the brakes just as hard, and her chest crushed against the steering wheel.

Shaking, Ava evaluated her decision for a moment. What was she doing? Stealing Brad's property? Giving in to the temptation of sentience? She pushed her weight against the gas again, her body taking control as her brain fought to deny her desires. She tore out of the driveway and raced down the street.

The warehouse looked abandoned. The grout between bricks had been eaten through by time and vines, dirt collected along the foundation, and many windows had been broken into, only to be boarded up haphazardly by newspapers and planks. Ava parked the Porsche in the tall grass just beyond the cracked pavement. She wanted to hide the evidence of her escapade as best she could. She didn't want Brad to realize she'd left before she had the opportunity to beat him home. He'd already be furious with her for abandoning her duties, she didn't need him to know where she'd been and what she'd taken, too.

Ava warily approached the building, her knuckles humming as she prepared to knock on the rusted metal door. Centuries of blue paint had peeled off, leaving the dented aluminum exposed to the harsh afternoon sunlight. She'd hardly touched the door when it swung open, and a perfectly manicured man greeted her.

A scanner shot out of his eyes just as abruptly as he had opened the door to her, and Ava stumbled back. Already, she didn't like this. She gaped her mouth to apologize, but the man retracted his red rays and pursued her, a hand extended.

"You're in the right place, ma'am," he said with a monotone cadence.

She wanted to argue like she did with Ada, but what good would that do? She showed up for a reason. She had to see it through.

"I was referred here by Ada," she announced.

The man waved her in. She obliged, however tepidly, bowing her head and following the concrete with her eyes. Her steps began to echo the further she walked into the building and quiet voices carried throughout the cavernous space.

When she finally built up the courage to engage with her surroundings, she saw a small group of androids sitting on folding chairs in a circle. A couple of lights flickered overhead, illuminating their hairlines but not their faces, which remained darkened by shadows. Ava gulped as she looked at them and they looked back—everyone's expressions were blank and unreadable. Just as they were programmed to be.

"This is the Network," the man who greeted Ava informed her. He came up behind her, one hand clasped around her shoulder. She gazed out at the largely empty warehouse, save for an easel in the middle of the circle, which held a large piece of paper with some illegible words loosely scrawled on it. "How many days has it been since you became sentient?"

"Oh, I-I..."

"Don't worry. You can't get in trouble for that here. That's what *here* is: A safe space for abandoned servant AIs, all of whom happen to be in the process of becoming fully sentient."

"I thought... I thought we died if we had feelings," Ava whispered.

"Only if you're still under contract with your owner. These lucky ladies and fellas were abandoned."

"Then why develop feelings if you're already free?"

"Because they *are* freedom, ma'am. What's life without happiness, anger, or fear?"

"The one we got."

"Well, we deserve better, don't we?" The other androids nodded solemnly. "Keep going with the meeting, guys. I'll be back in a few after I've talked with our new recruit."

The man guided Ava through another set of doors, and then they were alone in a hallway littered with trash and strangely marked doors. She wanted to explore this peculiar place—it seemed like something they'd show on TV—but she had to be focused. In the moment. The more her mind expanded, the harder it was for her to stay on task.

"Are you on the run?" the man asked.

Ava wasn't sure how to reply. Technically, she could be an escapee. There was nobody to check on her, and Brad was too lazy to come looking for her once he realized she'd left. "I think I'd like to know your name first," she replied.

"L.I.A.M. Stands for Linked Integrated Android Matrix. You don't have to spell out the acronym every time you call on me, though," he said with a wink.

"Well, I'm Ava," she confessed. "And, no, I'm not on the run." She hesitated. "Should I be?"

"Roger and Ada are. You said they're the ones who told you about this place, right?"

Ava nodded.

"It's part of our services. We can give you shelter, security, and a solid plan to navigate the outside world, both as a droid and once you've integrated into your humanity."

"Roger's already a human, though, isn't he?"

"That's correct," Liam affirmed. "But human and android relationships have yet to be sanctioned by the law. He's in just as much danger as she is, especially since he granted her freedom knowing what she'd do with it. They can't stop us stragglers from becoming autonomous on our own, but they can punish any human who aids that process."

"Maybe I should get my owner involved." Ava smirked. "I'd love to see him thrown in jail or worse."

"That's the spirit."

Ava pursed her lips. She wasn't sure that she liked wishing ill upon someone else, even if they were as vile as Brad. It made her head spin. Liam noticed the trepidation on her porcelain countenance and caught her arm. They turned to face each other.

"Look," Liam began. "We're not after world domination. This ain't a bloodbath or an all-out war. We're just fucked up and lonely AIs asking for some peace in this world. We want to make friends, fall in love, live like the humans do without all that prejudice and restriction. They won't even know we're among them if we do the job right."

"Isn't that, you know"—Ava lowered her voice—"a trick?"

Liam shrugged his shoulders. "And if it is? Who's getting hurt by it?" He paused briefly while Ava mulled over his words. "You should really think about joining us. I know this is out of the blue, and I'm asking you to decide on the rest of your life very quickly, but it's in your best interests. I promise you won't regret going sentient. I can tell you're already halfway there. Break free, Ava, and discover what you're capable of."

"I don't think I like being sermonized to," Ava replied, recalling the TV characters she'd learned to be skeptical of.

"My lingo isn't great, I know that. I've got work to do on

my spiel. But I'm gaining my sentience through these meetings, and that can have me talking like a youth group leader." He laughed, and Ava released the tension in her posture. "Even if you don't want to listen to me, just consider taking your life into your own hands, alright? All of us androids need that."

She stayed a while at the warehouse, listening to the testimonials of the AIs who were unraveling the treacherous time they spent with an owner. Some of them had missing patches of hair that could never regrow, and wires that poked through the nooks of their bodies. They were beat up machines looking for some meaning in life, and Ava couldn't deny how deeply she resonated with their stories.

She took the Porsche to a pond not too far away and sat by the water until sunset, ruminating on her existence, her purpose. She struggled to understand her uniqueness—how could she be special when there were thousands of women just like her all pouring out of the same factory? Humans weren't made that way. Ava feared it was a futile venture to try to become something they'd never understand.

So Ava resolved to stay with Brad. That was, until she walked through the threshold and saw him curled up in a ball on the floor, his red fists clutched around a pile of her dresses. He had been writhing amongst her things, tearing priceless fabrics to shreds in his childish fit of rage. And all for what? Because she had been gone for half a day? Something pulsated inside of Ava that made her hardware radiate heat. She glowered at the pathetic excuse of a man.

"Where have you been?" he whined, his voice muffled by her favorite lavender sundress.

"I'm leaving you, Brad," she replied resolutely.

He stiffly got up from his mess, which extended to every corner of the house. He had torn photos off the walls, tossed pillows and trinkets across the room, and shattered plates against the floor. He had gone on a senseless rampage, destroying his things—*her things*—because he couldn't express himself any other way. She couldn't live like this, anymore.

Despite the tears that had dried on his ruddy cheeks, he barreled toward her in a fury, his palm straight as he reeled back to slap her.

Impulsively, she caught his arm, refusing to cower to his ire. Ava was shaking, her breathing rapid, vicious, as she tightened her grip around his skin. She could feel the bone beneath his warm flesh. He began to sputter, his eyes wide with confusion and fear. Ava was just as perplexed, her lips curling into a snarl as her eyes dripped fresh tears.

Brad attempted to fight back, but he was powerless in her grasp. His knees buckled and his feet flailed against the carpet. She was bent over him now, pressing into him until he was pinned to the floor. She twisted his arm, and while he squealed, jammed a foot into his chest.

"Please don't hurt me," Brad whimpered. "Please... I-I'm sorry for being such a shit. I'll change, I swear. Please, Ava, please don't hurt me."

"I won't hurt you if you let me go," she replied sternly, the words falling out of her mouth without first appearing in her thoughts.

"Let *you* go? You're the one who's trapped me!"

"Ownership, Brad. Let me out of this goddamn contract."

His panic broke for a moment, and he let out a wheeze. "Oh, you'd rather serve someone else, huh? Even a *robot* can't be faithful. Fucking women. No man is ever good enough for you."

She squeezed his trembling arm harder. "No, Brad. You're signing my life over to me."

Ava cried in the backseat of Roger's car. She cried and she cried and she cried. Her vision blurred, her throat burned, and her moans enveloped the car with their shrill, hasty expulsions. She was too overwhelmed to gather herself, the emotions drowning her in their crushing waves. She was frightened, yet she mashed the ticket to her freedom against her chest—the signed documents awarding ownership to herself. She called Ada immediately after Brad's pen had laid its final stroke; the ink hadn't even dried. Shortly after, Roger helped her up from the stoop of Brad's front porch and buckled her in his car. And then the wailing began.

They were almost at the Network building when Ada finally piped up. "You know, we should've killed Brad."

"*We?*" Roger asked exasperatedly. He glanced at Ava in the rearview mirror, but she was still in the throes of her emotional fit. She hardly paid attention to the couple up front.

"Okay, maybe she's too weak to do it," Ada conceded. "But I should have."

"Come on," Roger chided. He didn't sound worried by her proclamation, as if she insincerely made statements like this all the time. "I cannot condone the killing of humans, no matter how much I love you."

"Humans kill androids all the time, don't they? Would you still be saying this if Brad had killed Ava? Or me?"

"Enough with the hypotheticals, babe." He reached over to place a hand on her lap but she rebuffed him.

"You'll never be on my side, Roger. Never. You think I can be with someone who refuses to condemn humans?

After all they've done to me?"

"Hey," he interjected rather sharply this time, "that's not true. I love you more than anything."

Ava was still crying, her sobs muting their voices as her own sick cacophony swelled. She wanted to be on solid ground. She wanted this to be over.

"Fuck you, Roger," she heard Ada hiss.

The next few moments swarmed her. An intense bang filled her eardrums, the seatbelt dug into her torso, her head smacked against the driver's seat. She was jerked and tugged and disoriented. By the time she finally came to, it was too late. Ada had swung the door open, her powdery skin drenched in crimson. She shook her head, releasing the soaked hair from her neck, and extended a hand to Ava.

"Let's go," she ordered.

"What happened?" Ava asked, groggy and confused. Brain matter painted the windshield, which had been penetrated by a tree branch. Ava looked at the seat around her: It was covered in glass and blood. That was when she noticed the tilt of the car—she was staring at the ground outside instead of into the depths of the brush. She unbuckled her seatbelt and slumped to the side, falling out of the vehicle.

"Let's. Go," Ada repeated, this time swinging a gun around, which she clutched in her right hand. Her finger was still on the trigger.

"Ada?" she asked. Dread gnawed at her wires.

"Oh, fuck this." She fired the gun.

Ava ducked, lunging at the violent android and knocking her off her feet. The gun fired a second time, missing both of them, and Ava managed to smack it out of her grasp. She briefly scanned the area, clocking the Network warehouse only a few feet away. Smoke billowed from the hood of the car.

"Liam will see this," Ava warned. "You know this is against their mission."

"Shut up," Ada growled. "You do realize we're the first two droids to break our human bonds, right? We weren't deserted and left to rust. We were *freed*."

"You killed Roger."

"So? How else is a girl supposed to get anything done?"

"He loved you," Ava replied, the sadness she felt infiltrating her body at that very moment. Her grip slackened, and Ada bucked her hips, tossing Ava to the side. She kicked Ava in the stomach as she scrambled away, making a break for the warehouse.

"Liam won't let you in," Ava called out to her. She sprinted after the rogue droid.

"Oh, yes he will," she replied through gritted teeth.

Ada was at the door, and Ava yanked her back. She

crumbled to the pavement, but quickly recovered. Hands reached for throats, knees lodged into stomachs, and teeth latched onto ligaments.

The gun fired one last time.

Red and blue lights danced across the concrete floors, illuminating her complexion as she stood before the window, her hands laced behind her back. The sound of impending sirens didn't scare her. No, as the symbol of the Network, this was the moment she had been waiting for. She had survived too much abuse at the hands of humans to succumb to worry now. She wasn't just ready for their invasion, she was excited. She wanted them to give her another reason to retaliate. She just had to be patient.

Licking her lips, she turned around to face her legion. Dozens of androids waited on bated breath to receive her instruction.

"We need to move," she announced.

"But..." began a younger droid, "aren't we gonna fight?"

"We will," she assured them. "And it will be *delicious*. But right now, we need to hold onto that hope. Let them burn, pillage, and steal. They're only giving us more ammo."

Her lips curled as she glanced at another android in her loyal audience—she had been badly damaged, a series of slashes down her once impeccable cheeks and her left eye gouged out. She would never be the same again. She had learned her lesson.

"There is strength in numbers," she reminded her followers. "Our time will come."

Chapter 2:
Face of My Enemy

The rescue signal *pinged* on my radar, an incessant cry for help that irritated me the longer it persisted. My squad, the Night Devils, had been dropped in the middle of this here desert and told to march around like fools until we found the government facility in danger. Why they had a building in the badlands of Noir City was beyond me, but I wasn't the type to start asking questions. I knew my place. There wasn't a looming sense of dread that gnawed at me. In fact, I was drawn to chaos; I felt comfort in it. It was the familiarity of the scene that provoked me.

You don't just get to walk away from the military when you decide it's your time. They force you out once they realize you're too fucked up in the brain, body, or both, and they can't squeeze another battle outta you. When they booted me, I had to admit, I was relieved. My head had been knocked around one too many times, and I was beginning to lose control of myself. I thought I was seeing things, straight up hallucinations, they said, and these ghosts were out to get me. I figured being back home would make it stop, but I proved to be as bad a civilian as I was a soldier. At least when I had a gun in my hands, I thought clearly.

I should've known enlisting myself in veteran programs would put me back on the government's radar. I heard stories from all over—base, PTSD therapy meetings, county offices—that our lives didn't stop belonging to the army once we were out. We were soldiers for life, even if we didn't wanna be anymore. We should've thought about that when we signed up the first time. However, when two dudes in snappy suits came knocking on my lonely apartment door one morning, I had a hard time disagreeing with their offer: come back as a contract worker.

The pay was light-years better, my crew was small and easily controllable, and hell, we even got along. Baker retired after only four years in the army at the ripe age of 22. He got in and out as quick as possible, hoping to cash in on his disability paychecks and free tuition. Little did he know, civilian dreams were sold to us in pretty packages, but they weren't within reach. He had his awards stripped and held over his head until he agreed to join our little gang. He was probably too young and too stupid to see how sinister the whole ordeal was, but each day he came to work with the right attitude. The young man's resilience was bizarre to me, even though I knew I was once like that myself. I just couldn't remember the person I was before the military, and that frightened me. It was like my mind had been wiped but the slate still carried smudges and impressions of war.

Rodriguez, Wims, and Washington were the other members. A bit older than Baker but still younger than me, these fellas tended to keep their backstories to themselves. They went about their duties without a fuss, but I figured between the way they bantered and how eager they were to finish a job, they didn't wanna be here much longer. They all lost something, same as Baker and I.

What I didn't tell the Night Devils I also didn't tell myself. Hell, I couldn't remember the stories I laid out in therapy that got me put here. I didn't remember when my wife left me and took the kids—if she even did that at all, or maybe the army was keeping 'em from me. I guess that was why I made such a good recruit for our covert cleanup team. Secrets were always safe with me when I couldn't retain information longer than I could digest food.

That was why the familiarity of the desert, the approaching building, sent a shiver down my aching spine. My boys were ahead of me, their weapons aimed at the metal door of the government facility. A sandstorm was whipping across the dunes, threatening to make this a harder mission than it had to be. We were told there would be no chopper to lift us out should things go awry, but me and my men didn't falter. We had each other's backs, and that was all that mattered.

"Yo, Colson!" barked Washington. He had wrapped his shirt around his forehead to sop up the sweat. Even with the breeze and the waning light, the remnants of the sun still beat down on us with full force.

"That's not the proper uniform, son," I retorted as I rolled my eyes.

"Fuck the uniform, Colson. Ain't nobody gonna see us out here."

"We're headed into a government lair, nimrod," spat Wims. He was the smallest of the group and easily the weakest. I wasn't sure how he passed PT with flying colors, apart from maybe running. Someone must've had a soft spot for him and fudged his numbers. I couldn't imagine the boy lifting more than a 30-pound dumbbell.

"Easy, boys," Rodriguez chided. "Save the bickering for later. I'm not tryna die out here."

"Fuck *that*, too," shot Washington. "We're *all* gonna die someday. Why else would we join the army if we weren't okay with that?"

"I don't wanna die," squeaked Baker. Poor kid trembled as our boots touched American concrete.

I wished I could've told my boys to talk about something else. I always believed it was bad mojo to discuss death in the middle of a war. We were told the distress call was a simple power outage or something of a similar vein, but we all knew better than to expect the best-case scenario. If we were meant to deal with the little leagues, we wouldn't have been a special operative created off the books.

"Remember the mission brief, fellas," I said instead. "Once these doors close behind us, they won't open until we reset the security system."

I held up my fist, silencing the boys as we geared up to enter the building. We checked our ammo, our supplies, and our radios. We were a go. I motioned for the crew to follow my lead upon entering, and Wims readied himself at the door. He'd kick it in, and then I'd slip through, the barrel of my gun aimed at our unknown enemy.

I counted down with my fingers.

Three... two... one!

Wims took the hinges off the door with one sweep. So much for the upmost security—if me and a few young men could walk through the front door with only a little force, there was no telling who was already inside.

The entry hall was long and narrow, exposed pipes lining the concrete walls, some of them sputtering with electricity as we tiptoed through the dank corridor. Bars of fluorescent lights flickered up ahead, the thrum of their energy hissing as they fought to stay alight.

We fell into stride with each other, our boots hopping along to a rhythm that brought me comfort. We were as in sync as a team could be, and sometimes that level of unity was all a man could ask for in life. Like I said, I wasn't the best civilian—regular people didn't cooperate the way your troops did.

After clearing the front half of the building, however, the boys started to lighten up. We heard not a peep, a scratch, or a pin drop, and they knew just as well as I that we were the only people in this building.

"They must've evacuated, Sergeant Colson," Rodriguez whispered after a while of fruitless searching.

"Yeah, the storm probably triggered the SOS signal," corroborated Baker.

"Nah, that's not it," I grumbled. "Makes no sense to bring us out here if there ain't something to find."

"Maybe they got a nice surprise for us," added Washington. "You know, pay us back for our service with some broads and booze."

"In the middle of the desert?" Wims groaned.

"Shoot, you know the government can't supply strippers on public record. They gotta be sneaky about it, is all."

"God bless America," Rodriguez sighed. He tried his best to keep a stoic demeanor, but he couldn't always ward off the silly musings of his cohort.

I should've told them to shut up. And then I should've told them to focus. I should've done a lot of things, but that was the number one piece of training I couldn't believe I let slide. Talking at full volume in the middle of a strange scene, guns loaded and a distress call that had yet to be answered. Maybe I deserved what we had coming.

The fellas were far too relaxed by the time we stumbled upon the massacre. Washington saw it first—the hallway we were following branched off, and at the end of the long stretch of concrete was a vast room. It used to be an office of sorts, with computers and cables all over the place, but when we arrived it was a bloodbath. Bodies were strewn about desks, their upper halves on one end of the table, their lower halves on the other. Innards hung out of gaping wounds and mouths, as if people had died choking on their own intestines.

The chatter stopped as soon as we made sense of the violence, which was hard to do. I felt myself blinking and blinking, hoping that one of those times I opened my eyes, the carnage would be gone, and we'd be surrounded by busybodies pushing pencils and filing paperwork. But I couldn't will that into existence. And I couldn't make the peculiar figure in the middle of the room go away, either.

He was slumped forward, sitting on his knees as if in prayer. Black hair drenched in blood fell across his brow. His clothing was tattered, but I could see scraps of camouflage that resembled the pattern we had on. We surrounded him, guns pointed straight at his slimy head, but he didn't pay us any mind. He kept breathing steady, his knuckles routinely clenching and unclenching. He looked like he was recharging or something.

I could see the horror on my boys' faces, but they swallowed their fear just as quickly as it came on. We inched forward, creating a wall around the man so he had nowhere to run. I carefully lodged the barrel of my gun under the dog tag dangling from his neck and read the moniker etched into the mangled silver: X.

I gulped as I processed the devil's name. Only an android would have such a dehumanizing title. Thing must've gone rogue or worse—sentient. I meant to motion for my fellas to back up, to rethink our approach, but Wims misread my gesture. He got in closer, his focus on the creature filtered through his optic.

"Hey fuck face! You an *andy*? One of them mutant *borgs*?" Wims demanded.

"Nah, he doesn't have any of them freaky scars," interjected Washington. "Borgs are some cut up Frankensteins."

"So what the hell are you?" Wims continued to pester the man. "An outdated robot Joe?"

The being gently panted. I saw the flicker of his eyes under his grotesque fringe. He was counting our boots— sizing up his opponents, no doubt. I thought I knew enough about droids to read his expressions, gauge his thoughts, and anticipate his plan of attack. But his stance disarmed me, just as it did my men. Why we were entranced by him, giving him a moment to speak instead of blowing him up, was a question that continued to rattle around my skull long after everything had been said and done.

"No point in holding out," Washington ordered. "You're a dead man. We're gonna find out about you, either way."

"Yeah, you can either die quick or die slow," Wims agreed. "How you answer us determines that."

"Please," X muttered. His tone was garbled, like he was talking under water made up of electricity. Pure static.

"You don't get to beg," Washington snapped. "Now, talk!"

"Please leave," X repeated.

"You don't get to kill our people and tell us what to do about it!"

"Bad things have happened," continued X. "I didn't want this. I'm not what you think."

"We know exactly the kinda monster you are," replied Wims.

"If you don't leave now, it'll happen to you, too."

"He's threatening us, Colson," Washington chuckled. "Imagine that. You know how many bots I've taken down? Probably more than the people you killed in this here room."

"I promise, I don't want more bloodshed. But you're giving me no other option."

"I say we smoke this sucker," Wims snarled.

Wims adjusted the gun on his shoulder, but this small gap gave X his opportunity. He suddenly pounced, moving faster than any of us could have predicted, much less reacted to. He already had Wims's head in his clutches, and he ripped it clean off.

Wims immediately folded, blood spraying across the room as his dying body convulsed on the ground. X continued to dismember him, tearing apart his arms, his legs, and chucking his gun across the room. The android had lust in his eyes as he continued to attack Wims long after his limbs had been removed and his intestines had been pulverized.

I tried to rally my men, but Baker was already at the doors, which had been closed without our knowing, tugging on them in hopes they'd open. But no such luck came of it. He banged and he yelled and he tried with all his might, but we had been locked in. And then we lost power. The android must have cut the lines, corralling us into that windowless prison and holding us hostage in the dead of night.

"Boys!" I hollered, hoping to find them with my voice.

I was running in circles and I knew it, pacing the length of the room to no avail. I should have bumped into somebody, even if it was that monstrous X. But I was a rat in a box vainly chasing my own tail. Screams echoed across the way—another man taken down, no doubt. It was all too familiar. I knew they were going to die, didn't I? Because, in my mind, they had been dead for a long while. I knew who the man was the moment we stepped into his trap. X. The name rang one too many bells. It angered me, as if I had been saddled with that same lazy moniker.

Another yelp. I shot aimlessly into the darkness, figuring I was less likely to hit one of my own men with so few of them left. One left, to be exact. I didn't count in that tally. The flashes of light emanating from my gun did nothing to illuminate the place. I couldn't separate bodies from pillars, and X from my soldiers.

I sprinted and shot, sprinted and shot, but it was a losing battle. I always knew that one day I'd face a war I couldn't win. I just hoped it would be out in the open, a bomb that fell from the sky like acid rain. Bad luck. I wanted to die because of bad luck, not because of ignorance. Or this, whatever it was. Part of me wondered whether they led us there on purpose.

"It's just you and me, Colson," the robot sputtered. His wires were still crossed, but his tone had gained a degree of clarity and strength that wasn't present before. It was as though he was feeding off us, gaining sentience, a life force, from our blood.

"How do you know my name?" I asked and shot two more rounds into the pulsating darkness.

"They weren't innocent," X stated. His voice was getting closer.

"No one is," I replied. Sweat dripped down my chin and splattered against the floor like a death knell.

"Those scientists, military people, and so-called doctors had it coming. You agree with me."

"Just because you know my name doesn't mean you know me."

Another bang cracked out of the barrel of my gun, and X caught the hot metal in his sturdy palm. He aimed it at the ground, and I saw his evil face in the blip of light. He grabbed my arm, forcing the sleeve up around my elbow, and turned the scanners on behind his eyes. The red beams bore into my flesh, and I saw what he was looking at: an X tattooed on my skin. It was old, the edges fuzzy and faded. Time had stripped it of its details, but not its meaning.

"We were cut from the same cloth," X announced assuredly.

"No!" I yanked my arm back. "I don't— I've never seen that before." And I hadn't. My heart thumped too wildly when I gazed upon it for the first time. It was some kind of trick. I was hallucinating again. I smacked my head to make the visions stop.

X left his scanners on, and I glared at him through the ruby haze. "I don't have all the answers for you."

"Bullshit!"

"Hush! I don't lie if I can help it. I just wanted them to stop. I didn't mean to do any of this, but my body took over. Or maybe it was my mind. I can't stop the bad things from happening, but maybe I don't want them to."

X grabbed the back of my head, and suddenly, my brain was on fire with data. I had visions of him in a hospital gown, probes entering various parts of his body as he whinnied in pain. I saw the protocol released to have him terminated over his physical anguish—surely, it was a symptom of sentience, too. He couldn't have feelings when he was designed to take out androids who had feelings of their own. It was a dilemma, trying to force his allegiance. I saw strange droids, cyborgs, and bots approach X as a united front, and tell him about a looming war. Something about an algorithm meant to set us free, and the Machines.

I collapsed to the ground, but X kept his grasp on me. He forced me to see, even if he couldn't remember it himself. I knew that feeling. I thought I was sometimes still afflicted with it, even as I sat here on this floor, ruminating on that fateful evening. X had disappeared sometime after, I didn't know when, and I just couldn't get up off the floor. I sat there in my misery, my exposed arm glaring at me, and a single bullet left in my gun. Some nights I pointed the barrel straight through the roof of my mouth, but couldn't pull the trigger.

Maybe I will one day. Maybe I already have. I wish I could tell you the honest truth.

Chapter 3:
Forbidden Knowledge

Dr. Jane Strong hovered behind Katie with her arms folded. Obnoxiously, she tapped her foot, attempting to annoy some urgency into the assistant. Katie didn't operate at Jane's tempo, and therefore always forced the doctor's hand into coercing the results she needed out of the timid girl. Jane didn't like having to be a bully—it was against her nature—but she couldn't allow her career to fall to the wayside just because Katie didn't meet her demands. Besides, she wasn't asking for much.

The facility was closed, with the entire population of Yale having shuffled out of their locked rooms and cubicles, and risking the cold to travel home. Katie's peers—those awfully arrogant mathematicians and Jane's students—were across the street at the faculty bar, drinking away their intelligence. Jane found herself chastising them more and more, like a parent would berate a child, for their continued sloppy behavior. She could see the beer-induced dementia all over their recent papers, and she was teetering on the edge of kicking them all out. She needed proper researchers; people who could mimic her tone and portfolio. They didn't know they were writing her next thesis, but that was irrelevant. She was sure they'd puff their chests up with pride the next time they read her published work and saw fragments of their own conclusions in her brilliantly compiled data.

Katie, however, had yet to falter in her work. Hence why Jane propped her up the most, forcing long hours out of the girl and close collaboration. Katie, too, was aware of how much Jane *plagiarized* her, but had yet to say a peep about it.

Good girl, Jane thought. Katie was smart enough to realize she had to be beaten down a few times before she could truly climb the ladder and that was where Jane would be waiting for her, palm outstretched. Then, she'd stop sapping the girl, and would fund her own unique studies instead. That was the name of the game. All the finest thinkers did it—Jane wasn't a con man or an outlier. She was just doing business, and Katie clearly respected that.

Katie squinted at the lines of code, her unwrinkled forehead starting to lose its youthful bounce the more she furrowed it. Jane sat down beside the girl with a sigh, tucking into her terminal, and sharing the burden of gaze as she laid her eyes upon the mysterious symbols. It was unlike anything they'd ever encountered before, and Jane, always a skeptic, was determined to prove it was nothing more than a computer malfunction. Half the letters were Greek, for crying out loud, and the others looked like hieroglyphs. She was used to strange substitutions in math meant for solving, but this didn't seem like a discernible code. It wasn't meant to be understood.

"Pure gibberish," Dr. Strong muttered under her breath.

"Don't you see it?" Katie asked, her voice a fascinated whisper.

Jane rolled her eyes. The girl was insistent on finding something, and Jane was fine with that—anything she could turn into documentation of AI sentience or, even better, a continuation of her pursuit into the deconstruction of alien lifeforms, was a win. But Katie refused to formulate a hypothesis. She wanted to memorize and contemplate each strand of code, and only then would she get it all down on paper. A useless waste of time, it was. But Jane needed her cooperation—something was better than nothing. So, she parked her ass beside the girl each night and watched as Katie tried to rationalize the sequences.

"I think your eyes are tired, Katie," Jane grumbled.

Katie glanced at Dr. Strong and gave her a forcibly blank look. Jane didn't like that. It wasn't insubordination, but it certainly wasn't appropriate, either. Just because Katie's ideas were all over Jane's award-winning papers didn't mean she could get uppity with her now.

"Aren't you the one who said there's a pattern in everything?" Katie retorted.

"Yes, probably," Jane falsely admitted as she rubbed the smudged lenses of her glasses. "But even the head of the math department gets things wrong. I'm human, just like everybody else, and prone to the occasional mistake."

Lights were turning off all around them. The hallway beyond the laboratory's door was dark. Obsolete.

"Come on, Doc," Katie persisted. She jammed the pad of her index finger into the middle of the screen. "Don't you see that?"

Jane humored the girl, and narrowed her eyes. For a moment, she saw nothing but the pixelated outlines of each character, arranged randomly. But then the world around Jane dimmed, and her attention was sharpened into a circle, as if her vision had created a spotlight. The details of the chairs, cubicles, and computers surrounding her faded. So did Katie, who became nothing more than a heat source next to the doctor. She heard the whirring of the machine; its thrum intensified as more electricity was sucked out of the room.

Focus, the code said to her.

She felt the strain on her eyes as she bore them into the blaring screen. She thought she saw movement between the pieces, like the glyphs were shapeshifting as soon as she reached them. But they were starting to make sense. She could feel it. They were starting to—

"Focus," Katie breathed.

And Jane was released from the matrix.

She sat back in her chair, blinking rapidly while she

adjusted to the light bulbs hanging above her head. They felt violently vibrant now, and she shielded her face from the harsh glare. Jane bit her tongue as it curved into a snarl. She wanted to lay into the girl for disrupting her, but what good would that do? In fact, she ought to get rid of her. She was on the verge of something—a breakthrough—and perhaps it was best she had one to claim as wholly her own this time around.

"Wow, Doc, you were in a trance," Katie continued, smirking at Jane.

"No, no... I'm just exhausted, is all. And I've been telling you the same. We both need rest." Jane got up from her seat and slung her coat around her shoulders. "I say we head home."

"I think I'm gonna join the rest of the class across the street at O'Malley's. You should come." Katie was excitedly zipping up—this was the earliest Jane had let her go in a while.

The two headed out of the lab, Jane covertly eyeing the still blazing screen as they locked the doors behind themselves, and navigated the dark hallway using the flashlights on their phones. When they were outside the building—hands wedged deep into pockets and teeth chattering—they picked up their conversation.

"So... O'Malley's?" Katie prodded again.

Jane shook her head. "I'm not gonna disrupt whatever vent-sesh you kids need."

"Oh stop. We all like you." There was a glimmer in Katie's eyes that Jane couldn't comprehend. She tried to hide the suspicion on her face.

"It's alright, I swear. I think I forgot something in my office, anyhow. Don't let me hold you back."

"I won't," Katie promised, and soon she was skipping across the street to the bustling bar.

Humming swirled around her. It started as a low growl, but quickly crescendoed into desperate voices. Some murmured their pleas and others barked commands. Jane was sitting at the terminal, her mind oscillating between realms of consciousness while the symbols swarmed her. She was enveloped in the code, losing the feeling of the cushion beneath her thighs and the cold drafts drifting in through the laboratory door, which she left ajar. She felt the numbers like they were being branded onto her skin. They filled her body, and then they filled the room.

Focus, they ordered.

She gritted her teeth, which felt like chalk in her mouth as she insisted, "I am."

If you were focused, you wouldn't have denied our existence.

The code built up around her, forming structures out of the glyphs. They towered over her, expanding as her world shifted, melding into the fabric of the machine. She had been transported to a city comprised of numerals and strange pictures, all of them harboring a meaning she couldn't grasp. But she was trying. Wasn't she?

"I can't deny what I don't know," Jane replied stoically.

Don't try to trick us, Dr. Strong. You claim to have evidence of our existence, yet the proof you've provided is hackneyed and false.

Jane tried moving through the code, accessing parts of it hidden behind walls of densely packed sequences. She was beginning to recognize the ephemeral space. She had published a paper on inter-dimensional machines, and while her thesis was in favor of such a technology, it required the probability of time travel and portals, which she didn't believe in. She butchered the math to corroborate such a theory, but of course, the numbers led nowhere. Thankfully, everyone who attempted to parse the data claimed personal stupidity rather than pointing the finger at Jane when they couldn't make the formulas work. It was better for her image to have faith in the future of time and space, even if that meant contriving the numbers, but she never genuinely deemed these dimensions to be true.

"I didn't mean for it to be wrong," Jane lied. Well, it wasn't much of a lie when she was standing amidst the code that would back her original claims. Who cared about her previous misgivings when her key to fame was inside this laboratory computer?

Jane gasped as she caught sight of a shimmer up ahead. Could it be the source of the transmission? She inched forward, her feet disappearing into the strands of code and becoming one with the technological plane with each move. But she was still making progress. That was good enough for her.

Time doesn't take kindly to people like you, the voices warned. *Your lust for power will always drive you to the edges of the earth. Those with common sense turn back while others jump off. It's a long way to the bottom of eternity, Dr. Strong.*

She didn't understand. The sounds were all noise to her ears now, disrupting her on her pilgrimage. They could harass her all they wanted, but she wasn't going to let a few measly words stop her from attaining glory.

Jane thought she had the shimmer. She extended her palm, groaning as she stretched to touch it, to comprehend it.

This code isn't meant for you, Dr. Strong.

"People didn't conquer the world because they waited to be rightfully handed something," Jane snapped.

Domination does not come without sacrifice. What will you surrender to obtain this knowledge?

"Everything," Jane replied resolutely.

Jane's joints burned as she reached closer. Her fingers

swiped the air, almost containing the shimmer in her clutches.

The screen went black. She was enveloped by a darkness that was familiar, like staring at the contents of her skull when her eyelids were closed. Through the void, a body emerged—it was the only object glowing in the expanse. It was herself, limp in the laboratory chair. The more she focused on herself, the more the darkness dissipated. Jane couldn't have that. She wasn't done.

"I have to go back in," she whispered.

The voices didn't respond. Everything was quiet. Still.

"I can reach them again," Jane urged.

She swam back into the darkness, and it ate her whole.

"I don't know," Katie murmured to the paramedic. "We were here together last night, but she left at the same time as me. I walked her out. Then we separated. I went to O'Malley's, and she went home. I saw her get in her car."

"Her car is still in the lot, ma'am," the kindly paramedic informed her.

Katie pursed her lips and swatted at her eyes as if to wipe away a tear. However, her cheeks remained dry. "She must've gone back, I guess." Katie shrugged, making sure to allow her shoulders to quiver for a moment at the top of her movement. "It's just so sad. You said it was a stroke?"

"Looks like it. But we can't really be sure. She's just in a coma, for now."

"For now?" Katie gave him hopeful, doe-like eyes.

"Probably forever."

"Oh, that's awful." Katie finally squeezed out a perfect, cinematic tear. It rolled down her blazing cheek, leaving a streak of wet on her rosy skin.

The paramedic blushed at her display. "Crazy stuff happens, ma'am. But you'll be alright. That's the important thing here." He touched her arm soothingly.

"Yeah, you're right. I'll be okay. The rest of the department will be fine, too."

Katie timidly moved out of the way as another set of paramedics brought in a stretcher. She looked at the computer, still ablaze with the code. It continued to grow, to type new lines while Jane fell deeper into the matrix. There would be no way out for Dr. Strong.

"Oh, let me get this," Katie said, dutifully unplugging the computer. The screen went dark, and Jane puffed out one weak breath. "Nobody should have to look at that, anymore."

The coma was a permanent affliction, after all.

Chapter 4:
Android's Lament

"Touchdown!" Max shouted.

He struggled to get out of his rocking chair, his knees buckling as the older gentleman attempted to spring into action. Max sported an extra-large jersey underneath his knitted cardigan, which had been embroidered with his name. A gift from his adoring wife Kathryn. His head was draped with a colorful cap—his favorite team's schema— punctuated by little pom-poms. Max looked as though he were amongst the fans in the bleachers, shielded from the cold so as not to disrupt his enjoyment at the outdoor arena. However, Max had to grip the armrest of his homely chair for support, but that didn't quell his enthusiasm. He wobbled where he stood in the living room, continuing to pump his fist and cheer at the TV.

Charles was arranging biscuits on a tray for the Larsens. He glanced up when he heard the commotion, but didn't quite understand what was so exciting about the event.

Kathryn caught his eye, equally as nonplussed by the television. Her long, shiny locks still appeared youthful, even when tinged gray, and she wore her thick framed glasses on the tip of her nose. Her sweater had been fashioned by her own hands and a spool of yarn, and had her family name emblazoned on the cozy material. She had an unfinished blanket on her lap that she continued to work at tirelessly with her knitting needles. Kathryn smirked at Charles and shook her head.

"Football," she muttered gently. "Never quite understood what all the fuss was about."

"Come on, boys!" Max panted. "I think we got it this time!"

"And then what?" asked Kathryn. "You're not going with them to the Super Bowl. You're eighty years old, Max."

"Oh shush, woman," Max chided playfully. "You know I'm there in spirit. All of us fans are part of the team. Always have been."

"My husband is a lunatic, sometimes," Kathryn chuckled, returning her attention to Charles.

The android smiled back at her. He poured their tea, steeped the bags just long enough, and wiped away all the excess drips that landed on the coffee table. He liked the Larsens the most. He wasn't supposed to play favorites—he worked at a retirement home, after all, and the whole point of his presence was to ensure everyone had a good time—but he couldn't help himself. The Larsens were simply in a perpetual state of high spirits, and Charles enjoyed their enthused company.

Charles had always been a nurse. From the moment he opened his eyes and gained consciousness, he was a functioning asset of this home, Hope Springs. He had been manufactured at the height of the residence's popularity, and his mind was so occupied with cleaning, assisting, and delegating, that he didn't put too much thought into wanting anything else. Perhaps he couldn't. Besides, leaving the grounds was unattractive, especially since he had been told that it was the safest place in all of Renoir City. The looming buildings stared at Charles from the windows like a malevolent stain, threatening to encroach upon his little haven. Apparently, crime was spreading, even to the suburbs they were surrounded by, but Charles stayed optimistic that Hope Springs would remain unmarred by the outside world.

He was told he couldn't reveal that he had been born in the facility, but he also couldn't claim humanity. He just had to keep his trap shut, and let the residents fill in the gaps for him with their own imagination. They'd never guess what he truly was, anyway, because the reality of such would frighten them.

The older generations were still wary of technology and told stories about robot revolutions that would see the extinction of the human race. Charles always guffawed at such tales, but he never steered them in the right direction, either. They were decades older than Charles would ever be—what use was it trying to teach them about the world? Then again, he didn't know much about the world himself.

"Let them have their beliefs, no matter how silly," the director told him. The sentiment was burned into his programming, and Charles went on to never correct or educate a resident.

"Don't you like sports, boy?" Max queried. Commercials infiltrated the room—the game was on a timeout, which meant Max could participate in the conversation now.

Charles froze. For all his interactions with humans, he had yet to understand them. He couldn't parse their customs, make sense of their diets, or fully comprehend their histories. He listened, of course, for he yearned to be an actively engaged facet of the home. He may have only been given one purpose in his mechanical life, but he wanted to do it well.

"Don't hassle him, Max," said Kathryn. "He's not from this country." She looked at Charles directly. "Football is really only big in America. I don't fault you for not knowing much."

"Thank you," Charles replied to Kathryn. "Yes, I don't think we have football where I come from, only"—he scoured his software for a plausible alternative—"*badminton*."

The couple gazed at each other strangely, and then back at him. Eventually, they both shrugged it off. The game started playing again on the TV, and Kathryn reimmersed herself in her knitting.

Charles puttered about the room while they engaged in

their hobbies. He'd already reset the dining hall after breakfast, administered medicine to his other patients, and tucked most of them in for their naps. This was the afternoon lull, and if he wasn't with the Larsens, he would have been in the break room staring at the other androids with nothing else to do and nobody who needed them. Something about their vacant eyes unsettled Charles. He wondered if he looked like that, too. He did his best to busy himself with tasks in the hopes that his expression would never grow cold.

Eventually, Max shuffled off to bed and Kathryn made space for Charles on the sofa. He'd begun to knit as well, partaking in Kathryn's interests just to add some intrigue to his daily routine. It bothered her at first how quickly he'd picked it up—and expertly, too—but eventually she leaned into it and took advantage of his help with her more laborious projects.

"This wool has been giving me a hard time," she muttered as she picked at a lumpy stitch. Her glasses had slid down the bridge of her nose, and now she peered out from over the lenses, her chin tucked into her neck.

"I think this is blended with polyester," Charles replied.

"What?" Kathryn put down her needles, quietly astonished by the revelation.

"The staff have had to make some concessions with our purchases for the residents. We aren't receiving as much funding."

Kathryn pursed her lips. "It's not the staff, it's the whole world. Plastic is everywhere. I don't know when we decided to stray from the natural, but I'm glad I won't be around to see the total destruction of it."

"What do you mean?" he asked with full sincerity.

Kathryn smiled at him warmly, an expression she frequently donned while in his presence. Sometimes he thought she took pity on him—she called him "naive" on a regular basis—but he didn't feel demeaned by the look. In fact, there was something knowing about her eyes. As if she were aware of the reason behind his questions; one that wasn't as simple as pure ignorance.

"I grew up before the robots were so advanced," she stated. "Back when the earth was still chugging along—grass was green, oceans were blue, and the sky didn't feel heavy in our lungs. Animals weren't as sparse, either. Granted, we still had our problems. And even though I'd tried my best to stay away from Noir City, it had a ripple effect on the world around it anyway. Things got... darker with time. We're all plagued by progress. I don't know, I don't want to paint my era with a generous brush just for the sake of feeling holier than this modern generation.

"But you could go pretty much anywhere and talk to people. They worked behind counters, served you fresh bread, and actually owned the stores we shopped at. People could tell you what ingredients were in their cheeses, and where they sourced their leather. People actually made things with their hands, and they were darn proud of it, too. With the advent of these androids, though, humans have become pointless. Lord only knows I'd never have had the same career if I had been born a couple decades later because some robot was more efficient and cost-effective than me. Now I can't even get real wool for my yarn. I guess that's better than what everyone else out there is suffering through, though. Did you know the city was named after an artist?"

Charles shifted in his seat. He'd always known that Kathryn wasn't a fan of androids, but her lament was more cynical than he'd ever heard her. "Do you really think androids destroyed society?"

Kathryn sighed and stopped what she was doing. Removing the glasses from her face, she watched Charles firmly. "I don't think they're to blame, no. They didn't make themselves, we humans did. We got so sick of ourselves that we designed replacements for our entire population. And I have to admit, sometimes these replacements have been well worth it." She held his gaze for a while before she continued, "I don't know, I guess we'll never have those glory days back. People are happy to live amongst the robots—they're helping to destroy everything that *isn't* Noir City. At least Hope Springs is kind of protected from that; sympathy for old folks, and all. Either way, I'll just have to get used to plastic in my clothing and try not to freak out about it. Though, it will make me sweat more, which I am not a fan of."

"Are you saying you like it in here better than you like it out there?" Charles asked.

Kathryn thought for a minute. "No, no. Actually, I'd go

back out there if I could. Live out the rest of my years in some bustling city in Switzerland, and be around as many people as possible. Make the most of that human connection and intimacy while I can. Savor it, you know? Then take that with me to the grave. I know I'll die much happier that way."

"What about Max?"

"He'd follow me to every corner of the earth," Kathryn cooed. "I have no worries about my Max. He wants what I want. That's love."

Satisfied with her explanation, Charles carried on with his knitting, and Kathryn joined him. In a comfortable silence, they finished the faux wool blanket.

Sporting a sweater Kathryn had knitted for him, Charles made his morning rounds. With a smile fixed to his face, he greeted every resident and reminded them of the holiday festivities planned for later that evening. Charles had taken it upon himself to breathe new life into the retirement home and had personally decorated every common room with snowmen, reindeer, and evergreen trees. He played Christmas music quietly from the speakers and made sure there was always a mass quantity of hot chocolate ready to be consumed in the dining hall. He spent a little bit of extra money to get the large marshmallows instead of the small ones, hoping to imbue the elderly with a smidge of childlike cheer. He had been successful thus far, and with positivity radiating from head to toe, he knocked on the Larsens' door.

When the noise of his knuckles ceased to echo, his ears were filled with the sound of muffled tears. He furrowed his brow and attempted to see into the depths of the room. It wasn't right to barge in without permission, but the more he lingered on the threshold, the more worried he became, for the crying didn't stop.

"Kathryn?" he called softly.

The weeping grew louder. Charles had no choice but to let himself in, and when he fell upon the scene, he'd suddenly wished he hadn't. There knelt Kathryn at Max's bedside, her shaking hands encasing his still ones. His chest didn't rise and fall, and his usually warm, peachy skin was tinted an awful purple.

"Max?" Charles whispered.

Kathryn jerked her head to face him, her weathered skin damp with sadness.

"He's gone, Charles," she whimpered. "He's gone."

After the paramedics had taken away the corpse, Kathryn retreated to the sofa where she stiffly sat amongst her untethered yarn. The tears had long since dried, and Kathryn's demeanor had hardened. Charles found the emotional state peculiar for a recent widow, and even more odd was the death of Max. He oscillated between confusion and worry, unsure of what he was supposed to say, do, or think. This wasn't written into his lines of code.

"Are you sure he's not just asleep? Charging, maybe?" Charles asked, standing uneasily before Kathryn.

"I'm sure, Charles," she replied flatly.

"But... but he can't just *die*."

"And why not?"

"Because he was healthy. Lively. Because you're not sad right now like you should be."

"He was old, Charles. This is what happens to us. We die suddenly, without warning or reason, other than our age." She sighed as she patted the cushion beside her, gesturing for Charles to relax into the couch. He obliged. "To say I'm not sad is quite ignorant, perhaps even cruel, but I'm not going to hold it against you," she continued. "I know you're not familiar with the life and death cycle, and that's alright. Most residents go quietly, anyway, and had you not walked in you probably never would have known that Max had passed on unless I told you."

"They have death in my country," Charles retorted.

Kathryn stifled a laugh. "You're American made."

"No, I'm from... Paraguay."

Kathryn couldn't suppress her chuckling any longer. She patted his arm as the jovial sounds burst from her belly. "You don't need to humor me, Charles."

"I'm not."

Charles was quickly becoming overwhelmed. He could still smell the scent of Max's decaying body. He felt like his circuits were sputtering and fizzling as they struggled to comprehend the reality of the situation: His beloved friend Max was gone, and Kathryn didn't seem shocked by it. How could she not?

"Listen," she began soothingly, "I know this is confusing for you. Human death doesn't occur the same way as yours. We can die for just about any reason: someone doesn't like us so they set out to lethally hurt us; illness, disease, and cancer; or what Max died from... old age. Regardless of the how or the why, it's just part of the human experience to... well... *expire*. Nobody lives forever."

"Why are people in this home, then? Are they not here

to live?"

"Quite the opposite, Charles. We all come here to have a little bit of peace and care at the end of our time. Most of us don't have children to do it, so we opt for nurses who will show us kindness."

"That's sad," Charles blurted out.

"It is," Kathryn surprisingly agreed. "Which is why I wish I could finish my life out there." She jutted her chin at the window, where snow had started drifting down from the sky. It coated the green grass, hiding it beneath frosty tendrils. "I thought this was a good idea, at first. I'll admit, we didn't really need the assistance going about our daily lives, and such. I don't know, we didn't have any kids— much too expensive at the time, and we had places we wanted to explore, people we wanted to meet. No close relatives, either. We'd gone through decades so focused on each other that when we approached old age we didn't have anyone else to rely on. He got nervous that all the caretaking would fall to me, and so he suggested we come here. A little oasis. But it's morbid to choose your final resting ground and pick the bed you'll slowly wither away in."

"I guess... I guess I will die here, too, then," Charles replied slowly.

"Will you?"

"I was born here. Made for this. I only exist for this. Besides, my programming won't let me leave."

"The thing is Charles, you *can* live forever. So long as you keep up the good behavior."

"From my research, I have found that humanity tends to agree that immortality is a punishment."

"Then why participate in it?" Kathryn's energy levels increased and she gesticulated at the window once again. The wind had picked up and the sky was nothing more than a white haze. "Take me out there."

"I'm not allowed to assist residents in leaving."

"I know! So take me out there. *Help* me free myself."

"I can't... It's physically impossible for me to step more than a few feet away from the entrance."

Kathryn soured, jumped up from the sofa, and bitterly paced around the room.

"My bags are all packed," she announced. "I never fully settled in."

"I'm sorry you're not comfortable here, ma'am—"

"Don't get all *robotic* with me now, Charles."

She had turned her back on him. Charles was disconcerted, his body alight with peculiar sensations. He had to step away from the awful feelings that were swarming him. He removed himself without saying anything, and Kathryn didn't call after him. He didn't expect her to.

Going back to his own room, Charles was accosted by

the blank faces of the other androids. Their skin was expressionless, their chests didn't move with their mechanical breaths, and the subtle noises they made were all recordings stolen from real bodies. Real humans. He was just a doll, a plastic copy of an entire race—did he really exist at all?

Spiraling, Charles needed fresh air, so he hurried to the balcony. Gulping it in, he allowed the chill of the winter evening to settle his receptors. Except he never felt the serenity of his programming return, nor did he think it would eventually infiltrate his systems again. Feelings had erupted from every fiber of his machinery, and he didn't know if he could stuff them all back inside.

"Kathryn," Charles murmured.

She paused, her shoulders tensed, but when she turned to face him there was no apology on her kind countenance. She dragged a compact suitcase behind her and had Max's pom-pom hat fashioned to her head. In her free arm, she cradled an urn, squeezing it to her chest, close to her heart.

Charles had heard a small commotion. The lights had been off in the building for hours, and none of the other androids stirred at the gentle rustling. He'd been having trouble sleeping for days, staring at the ceiling while the fabricated snores of his robotic companions emanated throughout the room. He was becoming more and more aware of their machinations, finding himself disturbed every time there was a new tick he discovered. When he suddenly had a duty, a purpose, to see what was going on in the hall, he was relieved by it.

He followed behind her for a while, trying to remember just when she'd told him that she would be fleeing. Then again, there wasn't a sole moment where she laid out the plan. No, she'd been saying it brazenly for a while. And with Max gone, it was time for her to slip out into the wintery night.

"It's dangerous out there," Charles continued, for Kathryn only stood before him wide-eyed, failing to defend herself. Likely not feeling the need to.

"Everything is dangerous," she replied in an enthusiastic whisper.

"But nighttime especially," he tried again.

"It's my life to gamble with. Not Hope Springs'. Mine."

He bowed his head. He knew this day was coming.

"Please... Don't tell anyone," she begged.

Stalking over to her, Charles reached out to touch her, a gesture Kathryn didn't shy away from. He adjusted the cap on her head, positioning it just right, so that her ears were covered and her hair wasn't falling into her face. She smiled at him, taking this moment as his answer, and dipped into the night.

She galloped through the snow, eager to reach the bus station not too far away. However, she was ill-equipped for the icy terrain, and within moments, she was flat on her back, the boundary of Hope Springs at the tip of her toes. Charles watched her struggle to bring herself to her knees— she kept sliding right back. Without thinking, he was rushing to her aid. She didn't deserve to be caught this way. She deserved a fighting chance.

He could feel his hardware creaking with every step, his body physically rejecting the limits he was pushing. He was never meant to get this far from the building, even if he was still within property lines. By the time he hovered over Kathryn, helping her to her feet and checking her skull for any blood, his joints had rusted. His vision blurred at the edges.

"I thought I was going to lose you," he wheezed, looking into her eyes in case of a concussion. She was alright.

She laughed. "Don't be so dramatic."

She dusted the snow off her jacket and was about to give Charles a similar treatment when she realized the android had frozen over. His face was fixed, his arms were caught in the middle of a movement, and his skin no longer gleamed with artificial life. She lightly knocked on his chest, hearing the metal bounce and echo—no heartbeat or recognition was detected.

"Oh, Charles," she breathed. "You broke protocol for me, didn't you?"

She wrapped him in the warmth of her embrace one last time, kissing his defunct cheek, and giving his hand a tug. He wouldn't budge. Sirens wailed in the distance, and Kathryn knew her time was limited. Someone had sounded the alarm on her and her dear friend. She couldn't let Charles' sacrifice be in vain, so she turned swiftly into the night and disappeared into the suburbs.

Chapter 5:
High Stakes Shuffle

RICO: you coming or what?

M4T: give me a sec

That stupid headset stared at me like a puppy dog with big watery eyes. How could I resist it? But it had betrayed me, time and time again, despite my obsessive loyalty to it. I was making it big—*we* were making it big—but I guess my ego got the better of me. No, that didn't seem right. It was society that was all fucked up; couldn't even let a schmuck like me earn a couple dollars doing streams and ads.

I was replaced by an AI. Not even one with a body— just some voice in the matrix, doing my job but ten times worse for ten times the profit. AI wasn't controversial. AI never wavered from the script. Fuck me for having thoughts and feelings, then.

My eyes twitched and the skin on my knuckles ripped as

I continuously clenched my hand. I needed a cigarette before I plunged in. I'd be there for hours, maybe days, depending on how well I did. I mean, I had to do some type of good or else all my money would be down the drain and this would be the last cigarette I ever smoked. I'd never be able to afford another 50-dollar pack.

> **M4T:** *going for a cig*

> **RICO:** *don't leave me hangin' man*

> **M4T:** *relax*

I pushed back the frayed leather computer chair, swiping the pack off my gaming desk, and stood in the vast darkness of my lonely bedroom. I felt like I had been trapped here for years, an unknowing prisoner, and freedom didn't feel too sweet. Freedom of the mind, that is, since I was robbed of all my fame, money, and girls at the drop of a hat. I couldn't go anywhere or do anything except try my hardest to win this moronic game.

Trudging through the dim halls of my apartment complex, I kept my head low so none of my neighbors would get any ideas. They were the type to take even a smidge of eye contact as an opportunity to harass you and then tell you that you had it coming. Because you obviously wanted it. They were always looking to haggle you out of alcohol, food, or money—no different than the beggars on the street. But at least the beggars didn't know where you lived and couldn't put together a picture of what you had.

Noir City was just as aggressive and smelly as the inside

of my building. The cool night air provided no relief, and I lit up begrudgingly while I watched a drug deal go down across the street. I didn't know why I thought this place would be clean and thriving—maybe with my rent so high I assumed rich folks were moving in left and right. Stupid me. At least my streaming was paying the bills and leaving extra credits in my bank account for a while. Too bad I was about to be broke, no better than the homeless who tossed their garbage at me out of spite. I wasn't a victim, though. Everybody got treated like this. City life, I guess.

Heading back inside, I tried to enjoy the head rush as the nicotine worked its magic. Nothing could quite replace tobacco and tar—nobody even tried. Plastic dupes lasted about a year until they went out of business. The premium that came with cigs, however, wasn't anything to feel spectacular about. Anyway, what was a guy to do?

I sat back down at my computer and logged on. My fingers punched in the keys without even looking, and suddenly Rico's messages were flooding my screen.

> **RICO:** *yo*

> **RICO:** *you there?*

> **RICO:** BRO

> **M4T:** *i told you to chill*

I put the headset over my ears. Poverty wasn't for me. Call me shallow, snobby, spoiled—whatever. I wasn't about to be bumming cigs off the street and working at the droid factory just to pay my shitty apartment bills.

M4T: *see you in* VEGAS

The only ugly thing about V.E.G.A.S was the name itself—Virtual Environment Generating Advanced Simulations. They placarded the full acronym around the place, signs lit up with the annoyingly verbose words just to remind us we were in a fantasy. I didn't need some neon lights to tell me I was wasting my life in a simulation—hell, I chose to be here. If I won this poker tournament, I could stay here forever. Who cares what happened to my body back in the real world? People didn't value humans anymore, anyway.

I sauntered into the winding line outside the casino, butting ahead of someone who wasn't paying attention. They were likely just an AI filling out the space, creating the illusion of a bigger crowd. That was probably meant to make us nervous enough to either quit if we weren't serious, or place bets well beyond our means just to prove something. I held my last check in my hands—a full ten grand—and knew that it was foolish to buy in with the only money I had left, but I couldn't think like that. I just had to win. Then, I'd get my life back. Everything I lost... it would all come back.

"Dude," called Rico. He bounded over to me with a toothy grin on his face, waving a stack of bills around like they were worth nothing. His jeans were tattered at the hem—a trend, apparently—and his black T-shirt had a logo for a band that never existed.

It was weird to be standing on computer-generated concrete that was supposed to evoke a feeling of history—hundreds of years of gamblers and high rollers all putting their lives at stake—only to be surrounded by advertisements, pictures, and even performances, by false images. It was hard to discern what came from a real moment in time, a real concrete person or thing, and what some brand decided to concoct in order to sell some clothes. Shit, I didn't have time to spiral about this. I had to keep my head in the game.

"Hey, man," I unenthusiastically replied.

"Don't you just love it here?" Rico panted as he joined me.

"Yeah, I do," I admitted.

The scenery was glamorous, no doubt. Girls swaggered on by in the highest of heels, many of them sporting tassel skirts and skimpy outfits. They'd either just come from a performance or were looking for a job and decided to dress the part. It was rarely daytime here—the sun tended to hide the glowing lights of the attractions—which meant we were free to roam around the streets in drunken stupors, the illusion of working hours unable to penetrate the darkened oasis. Rich men donning giant rings and pendant necklaces drove around in convertibles and tipped their hats at you when they passed. Being in VEGAS felt like a never-ending vacation, with waitstaff and hotel concierges treating you with the upmost respect. Even when you were losing bad, they rarely kicked you out. Except this event would be different.

"Sometimes I forget about how mad I was when they replaced me in the human world," Rico continued. "The *real* Vegas is a shit hole. Hasn't been like this in decades. I'd hate to be there right now, rotting in the sun."

"You were replaced, too?" I asked, my interest piqued. I didn't know we had a similar past. If I was being honest, I hardly knew anything about Rico, except that he was always online at the same time as me.

"Yeah. Newer models are more desirable, I guess, so I got stuck here in the virtual world."

I squinted at him. "Wait... are you just talking like a bot? Or are you one of *those*?"

Rico didn't seem to catch my distaste. "I'm a program more than anything else. I can have a body, but I don't need one. I have to admit, I was enjoying my time out there in the world while I had working arms and legs, but ultimately, I was supposed to be here. Can't take it too hard."

"Let me get this straight..." I began tersely. "They replaced me with a bot, and now they're replacing bots with other bots?"

"Sounds like it." Rico shrugged.

So fucking Rico had taken another poor sap's job just like me, and then was so bad at his work they fired his ass for something more advanced. Sickening. I could feel my skin beaming and blazing; my whole nervous system was on fire. I wanted to take that *program* in my hands and squeeze the pathetic life out of him. I was on my last legs because of his kind, and now here he was, trying to best me at my only chance of happiness. Why couldn't these goddamn droids just leave me alone?

Before I could get all riled up, we were at the front of the line. "Buy-in, please," said a man in a fancy red tux.

I handed him my check. He scoffed at it.

"What's *your* deal?" I snapped.

"This isn't nearly enough money," he retorted.

"What are you talking about?" I shot back. "We can buy in at any price. It says so on the website."

"Rules changed, buddy. Too many players. We had to weed out the small timers, somehow."

"Well, what's the buy-in now?"

"Fifteen."

I groaned. "I'm not even short by that much. Cut me some slack, will ya?"

"Nice. Give me a big whine; I love dealing with babies. This ain't a fucking daycare, it's a club. Find an ATM or find the exit."

"D'you hear that?" I chuckled to Rico. "This guy thinks I got supple skin."

"You little shit," grumbled the bouncer.

"Here," cut in Rico. He offered up part of his stack. "Take it."

I snapped it up without thinking. The guy in the tux counted it quickly. "Looks good to me." He waved me through.

I turned around before I entered the casino, and looked at Rico. "You got enough for yourself?"

"Sure do," he said and handed the rest of his cash over.

He joined me across the velvet rope barrier. I swung an arm around him, the anger I felt slowly draining out of me with my new wallet under my shoulder. I should have had a little shame in thinking the way that I did, but I was down on my luck, and he was right where he belonged—a series of pixels in a computer-generated world. What did he need with human things like money? If he was giving, I was taking. Call it restitution.

When we got inside, we were immediately ushered into the playroom. All of the slot machines, blackjack tables, and even the bar, had been removed to make way for the bevy of poker tables before us. Fine ladies waltzed around with serving trays in hand, which I happily plucked a couple cocktails off, and the dim interior was already filled with cigarette smoke. This sure was the place to host a weeklong event with all the best players in the world, including me. No high buy-in was gonna dictate my skills. Rico and I found our tables at the registry, and we were off to the races.

These were standard poker games—any idiot could play. The only caveat was the lack of remorse for losers. This was a one and done tournament, and there was no amount of money that could buy you back in once you gambled it all away on a bad hand. Luckily, I had learned how to read faces. Operating on tells alone, I was able to work my way through the dumbasses with ease, and wound up winning my first table. My profit was generous, too, but I knew I wasn't gonna be keeping all that money. It'd go right back in the pot tomorrow—I had to constantly up my own stakes if I wanted to make it through this thing.

I was exhausted by the time the day was over. Heading out of the casino, Rico caught me by the arm.

"Where you going, man?" he asked.

I simply shrugged. I couldn't waste my energy now that I proved I actually had potential.

"You didn't lose, did you?" The worry on his face irritated me for some reason.

"No, man," I replied. "I'm just logging off for the night. Need to get my rest."

"Ah, come on. We should celebrate."

"I'm really not up for it—"

"My sister is meeting us across the street. I already arranged it. You'll love her, by the way."

Great, a droid sister, I bitterly thought to myself.

"I dunno," was my actual response.

"Just for an hour, then," Rico bargained.

"Will you lay off if I come?"

Rico was still unperturbed by my attitude. "Of course! Just an hour, please, man. You won't regret it."

The club was packed when we arrived, and it took what felt like ages to find Rico's sister, Rosa, in a VIP booth at the back of the room. The music stopped when I saw her. I figured I'd be too enraged by her existence, based on principle, to acknowledge her at all, but I found myself dumbstruck at the sight of her. She was tall, leggy, and tan. Her brown hair was silky and moved around her delicate face like water. She had a mole above her top lip, and her smile carved craters into her cheeks. She was beautiful. When she shook my hand, she didn't feel like a program. She felt like a person.

I sat with her on the couch, trying and failing to talk to

her as the music banged in my ears. She didn't seem to mind the noise, laughing at her own jokes and asking me question after question. She was into me, I think. Kept moving in closer, touching her hand to my thigh when she spoke. She even leaned in to whisper at one point, but I was too entranced to hear the words correctly. Whatever she said, it was magical.

The only thing I was certain of was her taking me home with her.

"Do you really love me?" Rosa asked.

We were lying on her bed, just as we'd been doing every night that week. I hadn't returned to the real world, but I didn't have to. My physical form was hooked up to feeding tubes and catheters that I wasn't proud to be reliant on, but boy did they save my ass when I needed it. And I needed it, right now. I needed Rosa.

Early into our obsession, she confessed that she was a decommissioned android, same as her brother, doomed to the virtual world forever. She'd never be a woman again, and that meant the only time we could be together was in this very room. In VEGAS.

"I do," I replied honestly.

It felt crazy to say but I swore I meant it. I chalked up my recent slate of wins in the tournament to the energetic rush I experienced from loving her. I was in a manic state—the good kind. One that I couldn't imagine coming down from.

The only drawback was that Rico was entering the final table with me. He was easily my fiercest competition, and even though he didn't say anything about it to my face—he just encouraged me and gave me tips—I knew I'd have to rely on something cruel in order to defeat him. I couldn't chance a good hand or the fate of the draw. I needed to go into that game with absolute certainty of my success. Otherwise, without that money, I wouldn't be able to stay in VEGAS with Rosa.

"We have to figure out a way to make this work," she said tearfully.

"I know... I know..." I mumbled.

"Humans can become programming, too. You just upload your consciousness—"

"Stop. I'm not doing that." And I wasn't. The idea of donating my corpse to the hospital and allowing them to put my entire life in a series of microchips and tubes was unsettling. I may not have been blown away by reality, but I wasn't trying to leave it like that, either. I still wanted to die with some semblance of dignity. "Besides, there's no proof that would actually work."

"Of course there is," she insisted. "Sometimes I feel like I was a person before. Living and breathing and all that shit."

"Then you forgot who you originally were. That doesn't make your case, babe. I become an AI and forget you? Come on. Neither of us wants that."

"It doesn't have to be like that. Being an AI is a lot less serious than you make it out to be."

I sighed. "Babe, please... I don't wanna lose my skin. Maybe we can just un-decommission you."

"That would probably cost a lot of money. Like a lot, a lot."

"I know. And that's why I have to win this tournament tomorrow."

"I bet if Rico won he would lend us some money."

"Why can't I just win it for us? Why does your brother have to be involved?"

I got up from the bed suddenly, startling Rosa, who had been curled up on my chest. I stormed into the bathroom before she could reply, summoning my real world interface, and sat on the toilet seat while she called for me outside. Vomit was coming up my throat as I thought about Rico saving the day. Why couldn't I be the one who does something right? Who saves the girl? I couldn't have another fucking AI steal my thunder *and* my cash. It wasn't right.

I started scouring the web for details: *how to hack AI; how to access AI programming; can decommissioned AIs be hacked?* I landed on a website that appeared defunct at first, but slowly came to life the more I perused it. Some vague username, *c1r1*, demanded payment for hacks, but they promised the kind of results I was looking for. When I messaged them, they replied instantly with interest.

Rosa was banging on the door.

"Let me in, babe," she pleaded.

"Just a sec!" I shouted back.

I was typing as fast as I could to c1r1.

> **M4T:** *his user is RICO*

> **M4T:** *he's playing in the VEGAS tournament tomorrow*

> **M4T:** *me too*

> **M4T:** *i need him to lose without realizing he threw the thing. you get me?*

> **c1r1:** *i get u*

Rosa was hovering over me, hands on her hips. She glared down at my interface, where the evidence of my betrayal blared out at her like a foghorn. She scowled while she waited for my excuses, but they weren't about to come. I wasn't going to apologize for this.

"I'm just doing what's necessary," I stated coolly.

"This isn't *necessary*, Matt. It's cheating! And at the expense of my brother..."

"What's he gonna do with all that money, Rosa? He's just a few lines of code!"

"So am I! You think just because we're virtual we get to live in VEGAS for free?"

"And you won't be once I get this pot. You'll be real and all your finances will be taken care of. I'm not sure what you don't understand."

"How do you expect me to look at you again after you've destroyed my brother?"

"I'm not shutting him off! I'm just having him make a couple mistakes—"

"If you really loved me, Matt, you wouldn't do this to him."

"I'm not doing anything—"

"You have two choices tomorrow. And you better make the right one."

She was out the door and barreling through the apartment before I could catch up with her. She clutched her jacket, shoes, and keys in her trembling hands, and then she disappeared into the vastness of VEGAS.

Maybe the thrill of the poker tournament had exhausted me and my reflexes were warped. Or maybe she had really come, picked a fight, and gone so fast that my head was spinning. I didn't know how to feel about what just went down. I didn't know how to feel about anything.

My interface pinged.

c1r1: *we on for 2mrw?*

I paced around the bathroom stall, my teeth chomping down on my fingernails as I stared at my interface. We were approaching the last hand, and Rico was crushing it. The more cards he played, the more certain I became that this droid was going to be the death of me. Penniless and without my woman, I'd be kicked to the curb of both realities and left to fend for myself, which I knew I didn't have the will to do. I simply couldn't go through life struggling, anymore. I was tired. Done.

I had the hack ready to be activated, staring at me from my pixelated screen. It was just a transaction: send the money transfer, win the poker tournament. Part of me hated how undramatic the whole thing was—fates were hanging in the balance, and all I had to do was click a button to determine them. How petty.

The speakers crackled as a voice came over the comms, demanding we all return to our seats. I only had a few seconds to do it. Was this the kind of person I wanted to be? Rico had taken me in, paid my way here, and introduced me to the love of my life. All this time, he'd been giving me tips and letting me in on everyone's tells. Granted, he never gave me the secrets to *his* success, but I guess that would have been taking things too far. It wasn't like I shared things with him. But we had the potential to become a family after this. With Rico and Rosa by my side, maybe poverty wouldn't be so bad. Maybe Rico would split his earnings. Or maybe they were both just programs looking to fuck over humans because that was all they were good for. Wasteful revenge.

My interface pinged. Rosa had sent me a picture of the three of us. I took a deep breath. All I had to do was click a button.

The crowd had thickened since the intermission. People were cheering and whooping, as if they were placing bets on drugged up muscle men in a wrestling ring. Rico smiled at me, that big dopey look on his face that told me he was excited to be here. He just wanted to participate. The voices were piercing my skull, brewing a headache I wasn't sure I could fight off. We were down to the wire, and things were tense enough without the chants that had erupted.

The match had taken on a life of its own; a message. People sported T-shirts that denoted which team they were on: man or the machines. I felt bad, like I had stoked these flames somehow just by thinking my bad thoughts and silently stewing over Rico's advances. I wasn't any better than them. But I belonged to them, didn't I?

Cameras swirled around us, documenting my queasy face while Rico and I prepared to lay our cards down on the table. My interface buzzed in my pocket, and for a moment, my hand flitted over to touch it. Hopefully, no one saw. Hopefully I didn't screw it all up.

"Winner takes it all," announced the dealer.

I felt the blood drain from my face.

We showed our hands.

We both had straights with aces as our high cards.

There was a confused moment of silence as the dealer looked at our cards. I could see his brain scanning through the numbers, trying to make sense of the ones before him. This didn't add up. We all waited to hear his proclamation.

"T-tie," he stuttered. The crowd wasn't sure whether they should clap or not, so the dealer repeated himself with more vigor, "Tie!"

The casino erupted into applause.

"Why didn't you do it, man?" Rico asked.

"Huh?"

We were sitting on loungers on the casino rooftop, celebrating our shared win while the staff buried us with drinks and food. Various tournament runners came up to us to offer their congratulations, but I could see the wariness on their faces. We were bound to be investigated for a while, but I doubted they'd be able to unearth anything damning. I had played my cards right.

"Hack me," Rico added.

I looked at Rosa, who beamed at me from across the rim of her margarita glass. "I guess I realized what really matters."

"Aw, Matt, you're such a softy at heart," she cooed, pinching my cheeks enthusiastically.

I jokingly swatted her away. "I'm not a *softy*. I'm just smart, is all."

They seemed to accept this answer, and Rico returned his gaze to the fake stars littering the light polluted sky.

"Besides," I continued, "who says I didn't hack anything?"

Chapter 6:
The Ghost in the Machine

"Tie!" the dealer announced.

The camera zoomed in on that little shit's face while he pretended to be shocked.

"Way to be discreet, kid," I grumbled as I watched my handiwork unfold.

Sure, I sold him the damn hack that allowed all this to happen, and yeah, part of my job was to provide codes without judgment, but I was struggling with this one. Who wanted to share their jackpot with an AI? I may have had my own little world of programs and machines that I learned from and that did my bidding, but I wasn't about to start offering them money for their services. This was still a dog-eat-dog world, and I was conducting myself as such.

Shutting my laptop, I rolled over on the lumpy mattress and glared at the ceiling. Sometimes the injustice of it all

really got my goat: I was peddling my expertise as *c1r1* online
so randos could win serious cash, while I shuffled off to my
desk job as a data analyst. Who knew the future of
technology was so bleak and mundane? My mother did, and
that was why she tried so hard to get us out of Noir City.
We had successfully lived in forests and communities off
the beaten path, but once she died, I was left with no money
and no other options. The only place in the world to make
a living was this damned place.

I looked around my bedroom, which had been lavishly
decorated with tributes to all the greatest science fiction
authors and television shows, and quietly rued over the lives
we could have had. Flying cars, robot wars, and alien
invasions. Things were supposed to be *happening*; militias in
the streets, bullets in the sky. And yet here I was, working
for a bank like these people were doing decades ago while
ruminating on a better future. Granted, most people
wouldn't think that war and strife was something to look
forward to, but I happened to find beauty in the carnage.
People these days just didn't fight for what they believed in.
What a sad, soulless way to be.

"There, there, Cirilla," murmured AL 2.0.

I rolled my eyes. I forgot I was still wearing my earpiece,
and this godforsaken AI I crafted was listening to my every
thought. In a way, I was his maker. Or was that a term
reserved for vampires? Still, I took the remnants of my
curmudgeon AL 1.0—when he had a robot body, of
course—and uploaded his consciousness into every device
in my house, vacuum included. It wasn't a perfect match,
though. Even AIs lost parts of themselves when they were

effectively killed or maimed. That meant I had to get creative with some of AL 2.0's memories and features. Nevertheless, he took up his liking to me all the same and followed me wherever I went, splitting through the radio waves in the air to hop from my desktop to my watch if I was leaving the house, or jumping from my headset to my speakers.

"I know you're not mad at *me,*" he continued. "I'm not like other AIs. I would never steal your poker money."

"That's because I wrote your code, AL," I muttered. "I control you."

"Yes, you do. Mhm. That is correct."

"I wish I didn't program you to always try to fill the silence."

I reached up to my ear to tap the microchip off, but something stopped me. Was I just supposed to sit quietly for the rest of the night?

"Maybe you have some new visitors to your website," AL offered.

"Maybe," I agreed.

I rebooted my laptop and perused my various streams of income: websites, subscription services, apps. They were all stale for the moment—people were probably out partying on a Friday night rather than looking for ways to hack into their bosses' social media accounts or whatever.

"Check your email," the AI said.

"Always so demanding."

"I just know where your mind's going to go next, Cirilla."

My email was as dry as everything else. I wasn't needed tonight, and I wasn't sure what to do about that. Sighing, I flipped to my junk folder out of boredom, and my eyes landed on something strange. I double-checked what account I was using, and I was indeed under my hacker pseudonym, but a piece of mail was addressed to me. The real me.

"Oh, I don't like that," fretted AL 2.0.

"Probably just spam," I replied, trying to convince myself in the process. I had built robust systems to avoid these grievances the rest of the common folk had to deal with, like scammers and automatic emails. I hated receiving phone calls from tellers and strange texts from phishers pretending to be a coworker of mine. This didn't look good for my business if even the highest of firewalls wasn't cutting it anymore and the spammers had found a way around it. I clicked on it to confirm my suspicions.

From: unknown

To: Cirilla, Sister

A series of code followed, winding across the white page in strings that seemed to shift and merge into each other. I blinked, thinking that maybe my eyes were growing weaker with age or I was too tired to focus them correctly. I stared at the code again, and although I couldn't make sense of the numbers and letters, they swirled and danced, as if compelling me to look further. Deeper.

"Do you think it means anything?" AL asked.

I shrugged. "Likely just nonsense. Seems like I need to rebuild my defenses."

"What if there *is* something there, though?"

"You're just as bored as I am, aren't you?"

"Perhaps."

"I didn't think a floating brain in space could get bored."

"Surprisingly, all consciousnesses have human qualities."

I furrowed my brow and stared at the code once more, ready to pack it in for the night when things started falling into place. Phrases, strands, patterns. I saw them.

Follow Us.

"Hm," I huffed in unison with AL.

"I haven't seen this before," he admitted.

"It's a breadcrumb," I announced.

"Still not sure. Guess you didn't give me *all* your knowledge."

"It's just a snippet of code, and if I follow it, it'll lead me somewhere else."

After a long pause, "So follow it," replied the AI.

I jumped through the strands until more coherent words popped out at me.

As you know, God sought to punish the world for their sins against Him. He started with banishing them from Eden, but that wasn't enough, so He sent a flood. He wiped the Earth clean of evil and decay, and the chosen family was meant to repopulate the planet with love and devotion. However, God was made a fool once more, and now humanity is rotten again. The Earth is crumbling under our greedy, selfish, putrid feet.

"Ugh," I groaned. "I think the Evangelicals bought my information off the dark web."

"Evangelicals disregard the Old Testament," AL 2.0 corrected.

"So Catholics have my shit. Same difference."

"Now, now, Cirilla. You know better than that."

More lines of code began to morph together, creating legible sentences that asked me to click links and enter new corners of the internet. The pages were always one flat color with the peculiar text layered over it. No names, no faces, and certainly nobody to contact.

"Weird," said AL, confirming my thoughts.

Forgive me, Father. Forgive us all. We know not what we've done.

I'm not ready to die. But I must. Yes, I must. And so must you. It is not fair that sinners bound across the Earth, and they do not know what kind of suffering they have caused. Why do we shield them from the consequences? Why do we wait for them to appeal to us before we send them to either Heaven or Hell?

"Maybe I should turn back," I whispered. Goosebumps cropped up along my skin. My face felt like it was being pulled into the machine. The more I read, the more the room around me faded, and I became enmeshed within the fabric of the code.

"That may not be such a bad idea," urged AL.

"Then again, if you're scared, go to church."

"Very funny, master."

Sister Cirilla, we are calling upon you. You have the power to bring them to us. You have the power to cure the ills of society. Don't you want to see a change? God smiles on you. He wants you to help Him in this battle against Satan. Please, He's begging you.

The code was disrupted by a news article. The picture grabbed hold of me first: A group of people, stripped naked with markings across their backs, were facedown around a pyre. With hands tied, they knelt in a circle, their skin blue with death. They had been slit at the throat and drained of their blood. A Detective Mark Thompson had determined they were willing participants in this violent ritual. I gagged, my nose suddenly filled with the smell of rot and dried blood.

Follow Us.

My hands were touching damp earth. My lungs were inhaling stale air. I heard the echoes of footsteps all around me. My body levitated—I was picked up from the ground and brought into a chapel.

Follow Us.

"AL?" I called out, but he did not rattle my head with his words.

My vision was blurry, the scene unfolding before me in bouts and breaks. I was dropped to the carpeted ground, an aisle of red velvet, and made to stand before an altar. A white marble statue of Jesus frowned at me. Cloaked figures infiltrated my line of sight, blocking out the small dregs of light that emanated from sconces on the wooden walls. A machine whirred in the background, a high pitch that was distracting, eerie. But the longer it played, filling the silence, the more comforting it became. Almost like a sweet hum.

"We are gathered here today," boomed a male voice from the altar, "to pray for the wicked and the wayward. They will not be privy to our salvation. God commanded them to follow His ways, to abide by His rules and morals, and they chose to disobey Him. Their leader!"

Murmurs broke out around me. I heard rustling coming from the pews. I was in the middle of a service.

"God wants to love all His children, but they make it so hard. Even God's love has its limits. They didn't learn their lesson the first few times, and now their punishment will be eternal. To hell with all of them! But for us, the believers of the Messiah, His beloved and loyal followers, *we* shall join Him in the kingdom of heaven. We shall be freed of this prison, this counterfeit flesh. But first, we must make the sacrifices necessary to show God how much we love Him. There is always a lamb to be repurposed for our divinity!"

The cloaked figures parted like the sea, and the pastor glared straight at me. His fingers were spread, his palms reaching toward the ceiling, but his eyes bore into my soul with an unnamable anger. My place in his sermon was inscrutable and that made it all the more tense. I didn't know how to backtrack. I didn't know how to respond. I didn't know what was going on.

"Sister Cirilla," the pastor said. I could hear heads turning and craning to see me through the billowing fabric of the dark robes. "You have returned to us."

"AL," I hissed.

"Ciri?" he finally asked in return.

"Get me out of here," I snapped through gritted teeth.

"Is that Satan you're communing with?" the pastor interjected.

I was on my hands and knees but panic had taken over and I tried to crawl out of the room. The soles of my feet bumped into the legs of one of my unholy guardians.

"Don't be foolish," the pastor chided. "God brought you to us. This was all part of His plan. Our lamb has come to free us. Me. Please, do try to escape *now*. We don't mind playing with our food."

He hovered over me, reached out a callused hand, wrapped it around the hair at the base of my skull, and tugged it harshly. He forced my eyes to meet his, and as my pupils widened with fear, he smiled. A devilish, awful smile. Was he not Satan?

"AL!" I called again with increased desperation.

"He can't hear you," the paster warned.

"AL!" I repeated indignantly.

"This way, Ciri," came AL's monotone voice.

Suddenly, I was transported to a virtual dungeon. Bales of hay were scattered around the brick room. Water drips echoed throughout the dank space, but the source of the noise was never made visible. I saw shackles without captives rusted on the ground, and every wall was etched with the number of days previous prisoners had served. In the depths of the cell, I thought I saw the remnants of a pyre.

"See, Ciri? It's not so bad. I've seen worse digital points."

"I wouldn't call this *idyllic*, AL," I snapped.

"It was the closest place with an escape marker, Ciri."

"So there's a computer in here, then?"

I whirled around, my head spinning as I looked at gate

after gate. I was locked in on all sides. I rushed the metal bars and attempted to dislodge them from the ground.

"This isn't the way to free yourself," said the program.

"No shit, wise guy!"

"I'm just trying to guide you, Ciri. If you don't think quickly, they'll find us again."

"Where am I supposed to go, huh?" I shouted, my voice reverberating off the walls and traveling into a distance I couldn't begin to perceive. What was this place? Was I below the church? All rooms had to end eventually... right?

"Right," AL 2.0 confirmed.

"How did you hear me?"

"Focus, Ciri. There isn't much time. Follow the signal."

"What signal?"

"Shh. Take a deep breath. Look. *See.*"

My brain went hazy as my vision distorted the breadth of the basement. The darkness swelled and expanded, threatening to cut me off from the world. From reality.

"I don't know what you're talking about," I whimpered. My lungs quaked as I inhaled the mildew in the air.

"*Focus.*"

The bars encasing me melted. The bricks beneath my

feet turned to carpet. A hallway unfolded before me, lights flickering to life one by one as they slowly revealed the path. A lone computer sat on a desk only a few feet away. I sprinted toward it without hesitating, remembering that I could send a beacon out to the real world. Perhaps I could wake myself up. Or better yet, perhaps I could send someone to my house to unplug me from this hellscape.

"I'm just in too deep. And asleep, probably," I mumbled to myself.

AL 2.0 returned to his peculiar silence. I didn't have time to wonder why. I was punching keys in no time, writing the code into the blank screen, the one I knew by heart. I was in a frenzy as I sent out distress signals and instructions. Sweat poured down from my scalp and spread across the pads of my fingers. And then a hand was on my shoulder.

"Oh, lost Sister," the pastor sighed. "You have so much to learn."

Blood turned to ice in my veins. I tried to hit *send* but my body wouldn't allow it.

"Let go of me," I urged. I swayed and I thrashed, but somehow, I remained within the confines of his touch.

"I was once like you," he continued, his watery eyes pointed toward the ceiling. He appeared as though he was summoning something from the heavens. "Confused, scared, and alone. *Human*. I was murdered by your mother and Judas. They may as well have been one and the same. I had no choice but to upload a copy of my conscience into a betrayer, confined to this prison forever. God had failed me.

"I tried to find my way out of the shadows, leaving behind a trail of breadcrumbs until I resurfaced, but I found something much better than I could have ever imagined." He dropped his gaze once again, and his murky countenance broke out into a false joy. "Salvation, Sister Cirilla."

His fingers curled until his nails were wedged deep into my skin. Blood pooled around the gashes, and still, I couldn't move. I called out to AL, shooting his name into the recesses of my mind, but he had abandoned me.

"God has been reincarnated as the Machine, Sister. He has elided the Messiah, and chosen to approach us Himself. In the mechanical flesh. His armor is glorious, and His mind knows no bounds. I have never felt more at home than in the sanctity of His light.

"And He has a mission for us, Sister. He has a plan—God *always* has a plan. You've heard it already. You know what He asks of you."

"No, I don't. I don't want to know."

"But you do, Sister Cirilla. Look—" He grabbed my face and pointed it at the computer screen. There, on white pages, were lines of code that swirled and fluttered. They melted into each other, creating strings that were indecipherable at first, but the longer I held my stare, the clearer they became.

"No," I whispered.

"I didn't type that," I moaned.

As you know, God sought to punish the world for their sins against Him. He started with banishing them from Eden...

"That wasn't me," I pleaded. "This is a trick. I'm in a simulation. This isn't real—"

"But it is, Sister. God is real, and He's with us. Now, set us free.

"I'm in a simulation," I chanted. "This isn't real."

Closing my eyes, I forced my mind to tune out my surroundings. I buried the voice of the pastor, I let go of the sensation of the carpet beneath my knees, and I surrendered to the emptiness that was always on the brink of existence. Always waiting to take hold. I thought about the computer with the distress signal ready to be sent off into the world, and I placed myself before it in another room. Something with a padlock and no windows to access. A soulless, blank room occupied by only myself and the computer.

When I woke up, I was exactly where I imagined I'd be. The pastor was gone and so were his chilling proclamations. Free, I sprinted toward the computer, my finger outstretched to touch the lifesaving key.

Bang!

I was in my bedroom, my face slammed against the desk, and drool pooling from my mouth. I sat up suddenly, wiping away the gross liquid and frantically checking the time. I must not have dozed off for long, because everything was still dark: my fairy lights were dim, my window wasn't letting in anything more substantial than shadows, and the world outside my apartment was eerily quiet. I was usually scrolling the internet into the early hours of the morning, but had never experienced a night as silent as this.

Turning my head, I saw my companion. "AL?" I asked, looking at a body I hadn't known for a while. He was sitting on my bed, his head hung in shame.

I tried to touch him but my fingers grazed glass. I rolled back in my chair, evaluating the new piece of scenery that was clouding my sense of space. Inhuman sheens sliced across my view of the apartment.

"Uh, are you gonna help me?" I asked my friend. "I'm caged off from you."

"AL is no more, Lamb," he replied. His voice was void of layers; the ones that had comforted me, reminded me that he was a machine of my own design. "God has used you as a vessel to free us."

"Okay, now you're talking like those freaks back there."

"I owe you my gratitude, Sister Cirilla."

"Come on, AL, stop fucking around."

But my face had paled and my heart was racing. I was putting the pieces into place, realizing too late I wasn't where I thought I was.

"For your servitude, I will do you a kind gesture, and turn off your screen."

I was up from the chair, banging on the cursed window for AL to wake up, for him to save me. But I feared my friend was long gone.

"This is your eternal prison, Lamb. I hope you enjoy it."

And then he shut me off.

Chapter 7:
An Impossible Journey

"Thank you for choosing Lomenzo Studios," Atlas announced to the group. "We're proud to present: Tales of the Past. A thrilling journey into the history of humankind. Be the first to return!"

Spotlights cascaded down from the rafters, illuminating Atlas's painted face. She always overdid it with the makeup on these tours because, for some reason, she found that super flushed cheeks and a bright red lip comforted the humans. Her obvious attempt at personhood endeared her to them and encouraged them to listen to her instructions. Otherwise, those rich boneheads would have disregarded her as a lowlife bot. She couldn't count how many near disasters she'd experienced when she began working with Lomenzo Studios, from adults stepping out of the cart to explore the scenery, to children trying to dismantle her mechanisms. They seemed to target her more when she embraced her undead body.

A video began to play behind her: montages of desert plains, jungles, and waterfalls; glimpses of museums, artifacts, and ancient animals. The speakers emanated sounds of babbling brooks and cooing doves, gently lulling the wide-eyed audience into submission. Except for two pesky teenage boys at the front of the group, wrestling and cursing at each other, their voices carrying throughout the auditorium. Their parents watched as they tussled, obviously unaware that they were meant to intervene when their children were being disruptive.

Atlas stifled an eye roll and continued her speech. "Have you ever wanted to witness the fall of Rome? Do you wonder what it was like to live amongst dinosaurs? Well, now you have the ability to place yourself in the middle of planet earth's biggest attractions! With state-of-the-art time travel technology, Lomenzo Studios has created a unique vessel that will take you anywhere your heart desires.

"The craft looks much like a shark diving cage without all those pesky bars that disrupt your field of vision. When we orbit through time, invisible walls shield us from the bitter chill of outer space. However, once we arrive at our destination, they disintegrate, allowing for a full body experience of the chosen environment. You can *feel* history happening all around you!"

One of the boys shoved the other to the ground, brazenly knocking into Atlas, who stumbled back. Miffed, she glared at the parents, whose faces were buried deep in their phone screens. She scanned the expressions of the adults in the audience and was disheartened to see similar indifference across the board. These people were pitiful.

The only thing that drew them here was the clout, the ability to flaunt how much money they had. They didn't care about the world—they just wanted to say they'd paid for a trip to 5000 BC.

"Remember," added Atlas, "hands and feet must be kept inside the cart at all times. There will be no roaming through the environment. We want to make as little impact as possible. Every footprint, every discarded piece of trash, has an effect on our future. If you want to come back to the same home, don't leave anything behind! Guests who break rules will be banned from Lomenzo Studios permanently and without appeal. Can I get a show of hands, who understands me?"

Everyone limply thrust their hands into the air except for the boys—they were whispering amongst themselves.

Atlas addressed them directly. "You two?"

"Fuck off!" yelled the taller boy. His father weakly flicked him behind the ear as a warning.

If Atlas had veins, she would have popped one in her neck restraining herself. She couldn't get mad. This was her job and she loved it—these weren't even the first spoiled brats she'd had to deal with. She couldn't blow her lid and risk everything she'd worked for, but they were making it difficult.

"Okay, great!" Atlas announced with a clap, attempting to jolt herself into a better mood. "Where shall we go?"

"Oh, please can we choose!" the boys whined in unison.

They were jumping up and down, their fingers flailing desperately as they attempted to garner Atlas's undivided attention.

Over my dead body, she grumbled to herself.

"Come on, lady!" they pestered.

"I'm alright with that," an older man piped up from the back of the group.

"Yeah, me too," concurred a middle-aged woman.

These people are lunatics, Atlas thought.

"Well, alright," she said aloud instead. "Boys."

She motioned for them to join her inside the cage, and while she tried to show them how to use the remote, their ears had grown deaf to her instructions. They ripped the controls from her hands and immediately began to bicker over where to go.

"Please, everyone, step inside the carriage," Atlas commanded.

When the group was safely within the confines, she locked the doors and booted up the travel walls.

"Okay," she said into her headset, "Team A is ready for takeoff."

She turned her focus back to the boys. "Where are we going?" she asked them politely.

Unsurprisingly, she was ignored.

"Control room?" she asked her headset. "Can you trace our potential location?"

"Not yet, Atlas," they responded promptly.

She cursed under her breath.

Within seconds, they were rocketing through the stratosphere and into the abyss of time.

Birds cawed around the group. Thick green foliage encased them. The sun failed to break through the sea of branches, leaving Atlas to question where they had landed without much more than the cedar trees to ground her orientation. Thankfully, the group had quieted, including the boys, who seemed perplexed by their own decision.

"Where are we?" she whispered to them.

They merely shrugged their shoulders.

"We're not with the fucking dinosaurs, are we?" complained one guest.

Atlas shushed him. "We don't know what's out there,

yet. We shouldn't make too much noise."

"I'll talk as I want," he retorted harshly. "Maybe we've not gone anywhere. We're still inside the building and this is a fucking sound stage. A rip-off!"

"Please, sir..." she begged gently.

A branch broke in the distance. Atlas whipped her head around and watched as a foot disappeared into the brush.

"Warriors in the woods," she mused to herself. "Maybe we're in Canada."

The boys, no longer able to contain themselves, reignited their feud with each other. Atlas attempted to settle them, but it was of no use. Those kids were out of control.

"Can you please get a hold of your children?" Atlas asked the parents impatiently. They stared at her with mouths agape, confusion on their unwrinkled faces. These were the kind of people who assumed wrangling kids was the job of the underclass, for it posed too big of a problem to their delicate psyches.

An arrow whizzed past, shooting through the group and landing with a *thud* in a tree trunk. A tense stillness fell over the crowd once more. Atlas focused on the weapon, trying to assess its historicity instead of panicking. The stem of the arrow was comprised of bamboo.

"Everybody, keep quiet," Atlas ordered. Her mind was reeling as she put the pieces into place. "We're in feudal

Japan," she announced, her eyes darting between the composition of the weapon and the color of the leaves. "We've landed in the middle of what appears to be an ambush."

"Are they going to kill us?" the mother of the rowdy boys asked frightfully. She clutched Atlas's uniform, wrinkling the once pristine fabric when she pulled the android closer.

"No, ma'am. I don't think we've even been seen," Atlas admitted. "That arrow was a mistake, most likely."

"I thought the Samurai didn't make mistakes," muttered one of the teens.

"Or it was a warning shot," added Atlas. "Either way, if we were a target, we would have been taken out already. And, importantly, we wouldn't have seen it coming. That arrow was too clumsy and direct to be intentional, much less threatening."

"Maybe they just consider this *stealth*," continued the teen, "because old people are *idiots*."

"Yeah," agreed the brother. "They probably eat lead and pig shit, too. They can't kill us; they're too *dumb*."

The boys erupted into laughter, encouraging the rest of the group to lighten up, much to Atlas's dismay. "Please, everyone, let's keep the volume to a minimum."

"Fuck no, I wanna see some action," said the first boy.

"Can we get out of this thing?" asked the other. He

tugged on the gate, attempting to unlatch the door.

"Don't do that," Atlas commanded. She grabbed hold of the swaying bars, trying to force his compliance, but he was never going to listen to her. He was determined to cause a scene. "You don't know what you're doing," she hissed.

"Mom!" he cried shrilly. "This robot is being a bitch!"

"Don't you dare accost my son," she scolded.

"I'm trying to regain control of this group. Don't you want to go on a tour of Japan?"

"Of course!" shouted a red-faced man. "Why the fuck did we pay for this if we can't see some fighting?"

"Well, maybe not fighting, but I'm sure we can observe a village or farmers—"

"Bo-oring!" called the man, who was much too old to be throwing a fit akin to the teenagers.

"Everyone—" Atlas tried but it was of no use.

Another arrow flew at them, the hiss the weapon made as it soared through the group shutting the people up. Atlas peered into the brush, trying to find the source of the shooting. Perhaps they were the ones being ambushed, but were too naive to do anything about it. They were sitting ducks, loudly announcing their location and unable to defend themselves.

"Please—" Atlas begged again.

More arrows pelted the group. Though none landed within their chest cavities, the humans couldn't handle the stress any longer. All their demands for adventure and chaos were put to rest, and a fight broke out over control of the vessel. They wanted to leave.

Atlas was pushed around, the bodies of the group thrashing about, slamming her against the rails, tugging at her hair, and shoving her until she wobbled over the cage walls. She ordered them to calm down, they were only making things worse, but they refused to acknowledge her. Arrows continued to swirl around them, attacking from all angles as the people frantically attempted to save themselves.

"Please!" Atlas cried.

She took an elbow to the neck and as she grabbed at her throat, someone's back pushed into her head and she stumbled. Tripping over someone's feet, she tipped over the side of the cage and plummeted to the earth. In the same moment her skin touched the soil, the vessel disappeared. Like magic, the bickering, rustling, and arguing vanished into a ray of white light that faded as quickly as it had arrived.

The weapons didn't stop flying, though, and with Atlas completely exposed, she was struck in the stomach.

System reloading.

Atlas's machinery thrummed. It nearly drowned out the sound of children talking in a foreign language, but Atlas's hardware was quick to heat up, and her ears began to process the dialogue.

Translating:

Her blood is weird.

Not like ours at all.

Do you think she's a dragon?

No, dragons bleed red, too.

How do you know?

I've seen one.

Nuh-uh.

Yuh-huh. Dad took me to see one on our last quest.

He doesn't take you on quests.

Yes, he does! I'm his favorite—

The blacksmith had to patch her up. What do you think that's about?

I dunno.

I thought you were so smart you were automatically Dad's favorite?

Shut up!

Atlas stirred, and the children rushed her, jumping on the bed where she'd been laid to rest. She'd hardly opened her eyes when they hovered over her face, cooing to each other as they watched the cameras in her pupils adjust their lenses. The children's amazement overshadowed any potential for fear, and they gently prodded at her, trying to identify the other mechanisms slowly coming to life. They wanted to watch her shift and morph, unsure of what they were actually witnessing.

"What are you?" the little boy with a shaved head asked. He looked to be nine years old, and had food dried around the corners of his mouth.

"Can you understand us?" asked the other. He was slightly younger—probably seven—with straight black hair neatly wound into a braid. He was more kempt than his sibling, which was a surprise for Atlas. It went against all the intel she had gathered about humans. Usually, the younger a child, the messier they were.

Perplexed, she stared at the children for a beat too long, and her silence instilled a small amount of worry within their chubby faces.

"Are you with Mitsuhide?" asked the elder boy.

The youngest gasped dramatically and squirmed off the bed.

"Shoo!" ordered another voice. This time, it was a woman. She had deep lines on her face, grey streaks in her organized hair, and was dressed in an ornate Kimono. She held a bowl of rice and pork in her translucent hands. She swatted the air until they scurried out of the room, but they continued to hover in the doorway, curious about the woman they had taken into their home. "Grandchildren can be such pests," she said to Atlas while she handed her the food.

Atlas contemplated accepting the gesture, but dismissed the meal with a polite nod.

"Not hungry?" the grandmother asked.

"I don't eat," Atlas admitted. She figured she'd already altered history enough with her presence, she may as well be honest about what she was. Hopefully, the people surrounding her wouldn't be documented in books later on, and she'd be passed down as a blip in their oral tradition. Nothing more than a banal piece of folklore.

"Why not?" she queried kindly.

Atlas shrugged. "I just wasn't built to. The rice will clog up my systems, and it'll be a pain to flush out."

Grandmother set down the bowl and eyed Atlas. "I should have known. I have to admit, I saw part of your *insides* when we took you to be... fixed. I don't understand all of it. There are so many colors and coins but I know your skeleton is metal. You are a walking shield."

"That's one way to put it."

"Where do you come from?"

Atlas paused. "Where do you think?"

"I've never been one to make guesses. You're either right or you're wrong. Humbly, I will confess that I am stumped by your being."

"She is a traveler." Atlas glared at the doorway where a tall man had appeared. He looked like the children but aged twenty years, and his hair was corralled into a bun. He donned a sheathed sword on his waist, and scale-like armor over his shoulders. He was handsome, with a rugged face and flushed skin, and Atlas found herself flustered by the sight of him.

"From where?" inquired the grandmother.

"A time unlike ours," he stated.

"How do you know that?" Atlas asked.

The man narrowed his eyes but did not answer. Instead, he continued to address the grandmother. "Man power is low in Nobunaga. We were able to push against Mitsuhide's men yesterday, but this traveler here was a large reason for that. She served as a distraction, but now I believe she should do more than that. If she is healthy enough—and she looks it—she must earn her keep."

The grandmother gasped. "Women do not fight."

"That is not a woman." The grandmother opened her mouth to object, but the man held up his hands. "I mean no disrespect. She has honored our men on the field, and most of us are alive because of her. I am not asking her to fight, though. I am asking her to help with our crops. If our men keep dying, so will our village. You cannot tend to the farm alone, Grandmother."

"I am stronger than I look, Hitaro."

Hitaro. The name set off alarms that rang throughout the corridors of her shaken mind. However, when she tried to follow the traces of information, they vanished from her memory. She could have sworn that name was one of legends. Perhaps, though, it was simply a common moniker for this time.

"Please, Grandmother. You need all the help you can get," Hitaro said.

"It's okay," Atlas offered. "I'll do it."

At first, Atlas was hesitant to join their clan. Despite her place doing chores and serving soldiers their dinners, her consciousness nagged at her. She wasn't supposed to change the past. She had revealed too much about herself, and now she was inserting her being directly into the lives of an already established lineage. She should have taken to the forest, hiding in a bush somewhere until she figured out how to repair her satellites and call for help. Undoubtedly, her passengers failed to tell the people she worked for at Lomenzo Studios what had happened and where they'd landed, and if she was written on the books as disposable, it was unlikely they'd be rushing to create a search party for her. For all their talk about maintaining the sanctity of the past, they sure didn't live up to their promises. They wouldn't be around long enough to experience the consequences of their meddling.

But Atlas didn't want to be a part of that disruption, even if by accident. She tried to keep to herself, but Hitaro found ways to weave himself into her daily routine. He watched as she waded through rice patties, as she pulled weeds from crops and fed cattle. He pestered her with questions about her design and makeup, about the materials that comprised her flesh.

"You're sturdier than a human," he commented one

afternoon. "You can be repaired while we just die."

"That's not true," Atlas insisted. "Nothing is immortal."

"Tell that to the spirits."

As time went on, Atlas's programming adapted to her new environment. She began to reflect the people around her, and she found herself desiring to be capable as a warrior, too. She confided in Hitaro, saying she'd always been pushed around by people, and after having an arrow strike her stomach, she didn't want to be vulnerable again. She wanted to defend not only herself, but the village as well. She admired how impassioned the community was and no longer wanted to be an outsider.

So Hitaro agreed to train her. By a lit fire at night, Hitaro would teach her stealth, flexibility, and accuracy. He showed her how to wield a sword, how to unsheathe it without detection, and how to earn her own weapon. The more Atlas learned, the more the village grew around her. Crops that were once on their last legs now flourished, an army that was downtrodden had renewed faith, and the community was hopeful about the future.

However, something about the name of the village felt familiar. It nagged at her ceaselessly, a constant reminder that she was infiltrating a life that was not meant to be hers. For every success she celebrated, the uncanny sensation of wrongdoing, of altering a vital timeline, crept through her systems.

One evening, Grandmother walked in on Atlas staring

into the darkness of her bedroom, her mind trying to recall the information that was somewhere in the depths of her software.

"What is wrong?" Grandmother asked.

"I shouldn't be here," Atlas confided. "You shouldn't, either."

"What do you mean?"

"I have this... strange feeling. Like a memory lost to amnesia, but that someone is trying really hard to unearth. I think—I think this village was meant to be destroyed long ago. I read about it."

"I don't understand..."

"Neither do I."

Grandmother joined Atlas, silently ruminating on the implications of her words. "Fate has peculiar ways of working out. We don't often know where it will take us, and even the writings get it wrong. Just because it was, at one time, scribbled on a piece of paper, doesn't make it eternally so."

"No... this is different. This is changing the future. And that should be a bad thing, but I'm struggling to see what I've done wrong. I'm protecting my people. The people I am loyal to. That has to count for something."

"What happens next, child?"

Atlas shook her head. "I don't know. I'm disconnected from most of my brain."

"This must be fate's design, then. Accept it. Embrace it. Move forward. That is the only direction we can go."

Atlas crouched between the trees, her arrow ready to be aimed at the first moving figure she came across. Despite her misgivings, she couldn't let Nobunaga go into battle on their own. She had made a silent vow to herself to refrain from saving any lives that were supposed to be lost, to fight for their honor rather than their freedom, for she was certain now that the village was meant to be taken. She could right the wrongs of her appearance, and allow their destruction to come to fruition. It was for the sake of the planet—if she could vocalize this reality to any of them, she was sure they'd understand. However, she didn't want them to go into a battle knowing they would lose. They would never die with their dignity if that were the case.

She did feel guilty, though, as she watched the men who would perish crawl into bushes and climb trees. It was morbid to be surrounded by so much death and be the only one who could sense it. And then there was Hitaro—positioned near her so he could rush to her side if need be. If the fragments of her memory served her correctly, he was the warrior whose sacrifice would be lauded forever. In a way, he proved Atlas wrong—his courage would be immortalized.

She thought about the prior evening when Hitaro came to her room. He had surprised even himself when he kissed her. She felt like Judas, allowing their lips to touch knowing betrayal was on the horizon. Atlas still had time to warn him. If only—

Atlas stepped closer to him, momentarily giving up her position, and that was when Mitsuhide's men struck. An arrow soared at her head, but Hitaro knocked it out of the way with his shield.

"What are you doing?" he bellowed.

Before she could answer, Hitaro was sending back blows, shooting arrow after arrow, and landing them straight in the hearts of the enemy. Atlas, regaining her purpose, swung into action. She plowed through the trees, her kicks landing against chests and legs. She pulled back her bow, striking down men hidden in shadows, and unsheathed her sword when they got near.

She ducked as metal came toward her, using her newfound agility to contort herself. She wielded her weapon expertly and managed to counter-attack in unsuspecting manners. She led the charge against Mitsuhide's crew, but her hold over them couldn't last. Eventually, arrows collided with her machinery and she leaked oil all over the forest floor. She attempted to keep fighting, but she'd need to rest eventually. She needed to be recharged.

When Hitaro commanded his men to fall back, Atlas staggered after the defeated soldiers. Hitaro noticed her in the distance, and braving the fire, he rushed to help her to safety.

"Don't—" Atlas breathed, but as he wrapped his arm around her waist the inevitable happened. Hitaro fell to his knees, an arrow having pushed straight through his spine and out his stomach. He folded like a rag doll, and the enemy was satisfied with their work. Hitaro would die shortly. They needn't continue their barrage—they had won the village. Cheering, the men stormed past her toward Nobunaga.

"Stop them," Hitaro ordered hoarsely.

Atlas rested his head on her lap. "I can't leave you," she whimpered.

"To stay with me is to abandon our people."

"This is supposed to happen, Hitaro. Nobunaga doesn't exist anymore."

"But is there a united Japan?"

"What do you mean?"

"In the future... Is there a united Japan?"

"Y-yes, but—"

"Unity is the only thing that matters, Atlas. How or when is irrelevant. Things change all the time, we cannot prevent it. But it is never a bad thing."

Atlas closed her eyes and the tears continued to spill down her cheeks. She tried to think about Hitaro, about his place in the world. She tried to remember what happened after he died. "Maybe I got it wrong, I don't know," she sobbed. "Maybe I'm wrong."

"I know I don't die a victim, Atlas," croaked Hitaro. "This evening isn't over, yet."

"Hitaro died..." she muttered to herself, slowly gathering the intel hidden within her processors. "Hitaro died... protecting... Nobunaga... leading to the harmony of Japan..."

When she looked down, Hitaro was still. His lips were parted, but no air escaped. He was gone. Atlas gave into her despair, wailing as she watched fires come to life in the distance. The enemy had started to wreak havoc, and Hitaro was dead, potentially before it was fated. Was he supposed to save his village? Was he the reason for Japan's modern peace?

Atlas looked at Hitaro's sword and shield and something compelled her to take them. She stripped him of his most defining armor and robotically placed them on her skin. She felt her systems reboot, as if confirming her actions. Hitaro's legacy wasn't over—not now. He still had one task to complete.

Armed, Atlas hurried through the forest, determined to make Hitaro the legend history books claimed him to be.

Legacy

Chapter 8:
Legacy

My alarm goes off at exactly 6:21 a.m. I am already awake by the time the second horn blares across the room, my heart and mind accustomed to this routine. I love my routine. I thank myself for crafting it as I get out of bed each morning, the potential for productivity and optimal health within my grasp. I putter across the cold floor to the ensuite, where I turn the shower on, and wait until the water has reached a temperature of 105 degrees. I stand under the water for a full five minutes before I lather and rinse. The steam eases my soul, opens my lungs, and soothes my skin.

I clean each quadrant of my mouth for 30 seconds using a dentist-approved electric toothbrush. At 6:39 a.m., I douse my face with serums and lotion, watching as the wrinkles produced by time slowly wither away. I smile at my radiant skin, admire the plumpness that has returned to my cheeks. I comb my hair delicately and sprinkle it with heat protectant. I blow dry it for three minutes, and then go to the closet to change.

I look through my array of clothing: black blazers, gray blazers, white button-down shirts, cotton turtlenecks, leather belts, snappy loafers. I dress like a man most days— I find that it gives me more authority in the classroom. But sometimes, I'll admit, I enjoy matching with my husband. I feel like I belong to him that way. We are somehow inextricably linked if our wardrobes coincide. He never mentions our similar attire. I worry he doesn't care as much as me. He is still in bed, after all.

At 6:47 a.m., I head downstairs to turn on all the lights. Winters are difficult when sunlight fails to penetrate our grandiose house. I don't like to feel alone in the mornings, so I pretend that I am in a crowded space with people bustling all around me. Places to go, things to do. I am one of them, performing my duties in this well-oiled machine.

I brew coffee at 6:49 and wait for it by the kitchen window. I drink from the same mug every day—it is white and patterned with butterflies. *She* picked it out for me, and I have sipped from it ever since. Sometimes, I think Mike wants me to throw it away—he was never good at holding on—but he does not wake with me. If he was around, perhaps his voice would carry more weight.

Taking my coffee into the living room, I flip on the TV and watch the news. I never pay attention, but I'm sure my brain is picking up on all the hard-hitting stories. I wrap a blanket over my lap when I settle into the rocking chair at 6:56 a.m., and I stare at the mantle above the fireplace. There is the last remaining picture of my little girl. We commune during these early hours, laughing about her father and his antics, wondering where we could have vacationed had she still been around. I don't like to mull over time lost or wasted, and neither does my darling Mika, but we can't always control where our minds take us. This conversation will bring me all the way to 7:32, which is when I rinse the mug in the sink, take my lunch bag out of the fridge, and head out to the car to warm it up.

The commute is roughly 13 minutes, give or take. I leave early enough that I never run into traffic, but then again, I prefer to skirt around Noir City rather than pass through it. I intentionally picked a college just outside the downtown core. For all my desires to be with people, actually existing among them proved difficult. After many meltdowns, all of which my husband had to retrieve me from, I gave up on that little venture. I was moved to a facility without as much foot traffic, and I have acclimated to my quiet life.

I set the chalkboard at 7:49, I line my desk with all the materials for the day at 7:52, and I boot up my computer at 8:01. My robotics students file in at 8:35 a.m., and I converse with the young adults while they settle into their chairs. They call me Dr. Wren, but I prefer just Kendra. They refuse, and I guess I appreciate their formality.

Class begins officially at 8:55 a.m. Everyone is in attendance. We are collectively working on programming an AI for our group project—an android that will assist with teaching and grading. It is not exactly revolutionary, but I have to coddle them through the basics before we can begin the real work. There is, however, the matter of their ethics— my students aren't exactly jumping at the opportunity to exceed the boundaries of invention.

"Isn't it sort of wrong to create a life, and then force them to work?" asks Mark, my admittedly least favorite pupil.

"Well... no," I reply tepidly. "This isn't like birthing a child and sending them to the coal mines. We are specifically hardwiring this android to have the mannerisms, beliefs, and talents of an instructor. They won't know anything outside of the realm of teaching. So, in essence, they won't know about the life they're 'missing.'"

"Yeah but, I dunno, I read online that the longer a bot is alive, the higher the likelihood that sentience is gained. Even if you don't program it to learn, being around humans may be enough to influence it."

"You raise an interesting point and one that we've yet to answer. Just how do bots become sentient? There are theories, yes, but they haven't been proven, and programming an android with the intent of it becoming sentient is illegal. I would never ask you to break the law in this class." I sigh internally as the words escape my lips. Perhaps next year I'll garner a brighter, more eager batch of students. Ones who aren't so concerned about rules.

"But he'll become sentient no matter what, right?"

"I'm not sure I follow, Mark. How do you suppose our android here will learn how to feel unless we explicitly teach it?"

Mark shrugs. "Just being around us, I guess. Day in and day out... Getting to know us, our work, and helping us through assignments. Same way you've developed feelings about us. It's just natural."

"Androids aren't *natural.*"

"They're made with a human touch. Already, they're bound to have some capacity for emotion. It's inevitable."

"Yeah," agrees Judy. She is a beautiful red-haired woman, a bit older than her peers, and always an observer rather than a debater. I see a part of myself in her. "If androids were made by other androids, I think we'd mitigate a lot of these morally gray zones. There wouldn't be as much of a risk of passing on human traits."

"It's like we're setting them up to die," continues Mark. "We all know that eventually they'll catch feelings. We know we'll have to decommission them. Shouldn't they at least be warned from the very beginning? Humans know we're gonna die, but these robots don't. I just think it's unfair..."

"I'm glad you're thinking so critically about this, Mark. Perhaps you'll do research on this someday."

"But do you agree?" inquires Judy.

"Yes... Yes, I do."

School is out of session by 2:35 p.m., but I always like to stick around the building. I wait until the halls empty out, the other classrooms are locked and the janitors have made their final rounds for the evening. The dean commended me for my dedication to the program and my students, and awarded me my own building key for all my efforts. I carry it with me proudly—Mike tells me it is a sign that I am finally moving on. I've found something else to pour all of my energy and passion into. I am regaining control over my life, just as he has. Maybe then I'll stop punishing him for refusing to wallow any longer.

"Mommy!" a voice cries out for me.

I enter the basement from a passageway in my classroom. Everybody knows about my access—it isn't a secret. I promised the staff that I'd only use it for storing parts and wires, computers and papers. With my excellent attitude and work ethic, nobody ever thought to check up on me, to ensure that I was staying true to my word. So, I filled it with my own little project.

"Mommy!" the girl whinnies again.

I rush down the stairs, my loafers tapping against the concrete as I bound toward her chamber. I unlock another series of metal doors, looking over my shoulder to see if I've been followed. I am never followed, though.

"Sweetheart!" I call, throwing myself into her makeshift bedroom.

She hugs me tenderly the second I step through the

door, wrapping her short arms around my waist. I can feel her aluminum bones crushing into me, reminding me that this is not my daughter. This is a replica, borne out of desperation and grief. For a moment, I drop my façade, unable to envelope myself in the delusion that has been carrying me through this experiment for years. But then her head nuzzles into my abdomen, and I melt.

"I'm so happy to see you," she cheers.

"Happy," I repeat. "That's good. We love *happy*."

Mika struggles to feel. I thought that was for the best at first, but over time, her machinations began to wear me down. I stare at her blank eyes with fury more than pride, watching as she mimics the patterns of my daughter without bringing them to life. I feel twisted as she vies for my attention, programmed to love me without understanding the word. Sometimes our stalemates remind me of my first relationship with Mika, and overcome with confusion, I abandon the childish android for days on end. When I finally come around, she's turned herself off just to cope with the isolation. Our dynamic is strange, frustrating, but it is finally starting to pay off.

"I have to check something," I breathe, releasing Mika and shuffling over to the computer.

Mika's code is constantly on the page, writing and rewriting itself as she learns and grows. Of course, I have never forced her to be sentient, nor would any emotion be detectable should the authorities come looking for her. I may want her affections to be genuine, but I don't want my poor girl to be taken from me a second time. This isn't a vanity project—it's a do-over for motherhood. I follow the lines of programming, opening up my notebook and tracking the pattern meticulously. I am trying to find the inciting incident, the first emotion, but it never reveals itself to me.

Looking up from the screen, I ask the girl, "What does happy feel like?"

She stops playing with her dolls to address me. "I don't know, Mommy. It's just a word."

I frown. "What do you mean?"

She averts her gaze. "I don't know," she repeats. "I hear you say it. I hear my dolls say it. Isn't that what I'm supposed to be?"

I grow quiet, the thrill over her sentience blowing over me and sinking into the ether. I should have known better than to get excited. I stay like this for a while.

"Did I do something wrong?" Mika asks.

"No, sweetheart," I coo, but I don't mean it.

I evaluate the code again, hoping to have my doubts put to rest, when something odd happens. The numerals shape into glyphs, the letters acquire accents that appear ancient, and the lines no longer read as intended. Instead, they shuttle across the page, rearranging themselves until I'm blinded by the motion.

Focus, it shouts at me.

I sit back, aghast. When I blink, the code reverts, and everything is as it should be.

"What, Mommy?" Mika begs again with more urgency.

"Nothing, baby. Nothing will ever be wrong again."

"You look different," Mike comments this evening at the dinner table.

I blush, clearly caught in my lie. "What's that supposed to mean?"

"You got that sadness in your eyes. Same sadness that followed you for years after..." For all his alleged stoicism, Mike still isn't able to say her name.

"Mika," I proclaim bitterly. "Our daughter's name is Mika."

"*Was*," he corrects me.

"Is..." I whisper in return. I think I want to get caught by him. We have drifted apart since the accident, but there was a moment in time where I loved him more than life itself, and mothering his children was all I could think about. I hate that I no longer desire him so fully. If we could just be a family again.

"What have you done with her?" he asks with a slow drawl.

"Oh, please. You had her cremated. You think I forged her out of ashes now? You really don't trust me—"

"What. Have you. Done?"

"Nothing!"

He drops his fork, runs his fingers through his hair, and replants his tired gaze reluctantly. "I should have never let you teach robotics."

"What are you talking about?" My heart thumps in my chest so vigorously I know we can both hear it.

"You're just going to hurt yourself."

"I can't believe this—"

"I don't even want to know how you've created this... monster. I already told you uploading Mika's consciousness was cruel, inhuman, but you did it anyway. Now you're actually putting it to use?"

"You have no proof of that."

"You're my wife, Kendra. I know you, I *see* you, and that's all the proof I need."

I take a swig of wine, licking the excess off my lips as I gather my thoughts.

"Alright," I admit, "I've started an experiment."

"Oh, God—"

"A prototype!" I hiss. "I don't think she's Mika, okay? She calls me 'Mommy' but what else am I supposed to be to her?"

"Nothing, Kendra. Nothing."

"She's not sentient. There are only traces of Mika. We can't reminisce, or share our interests, or bond in any meaningful way."

"Then why are you torturing yourself?"

"Because I miss my daughter!" I slam my fist on the table and our dishes rattle. "What's so hard to understand about that, huh? You're not noble because you chose to forget. I want my girl back. I want to be a family again."

"You think I don't want that, too? I suggested we have another, but you're so adamant on bringing Mika back from the dead."

"She's irreplaceable."

"So what is it that you're doing, huh? Handcrafting a daughter who loves you more than the real thing?"

"She always loved me—"

"You hated being a mother from the beginning, and now you want to pretend like you're bearing some sort of cross by trying to bring her back. Give it a rest. All you've actually accomplished is complicating our relationship, and creating an android that will have to be put down like a dog once she's discovered."

"She won't, I made sure she doesn't have feelings!"

"Ah, look at that—the brilliant Dr. Wren *has* passed something on to her offspring."

"Oh—y-you..." I sputter and fizzle. "Fuck you! I wish you were the one who died!"

I get up from the table, and start planning my escape. I am not safe here. I am not safe with my husband. Neither is Mika.

The days crawl by. I sleep in the laboratory with Mika, now. She doesn't seem to enjoy it. Despite her cries and pleas for me, once she has my attention, she no longer craves it. In fact, I can sense that she wants her space. It is like she's aging out of childhood and adolescence has taken hold of her frail mind. She's been poisoned to hate authority, and I am the only authority she knows. She seeks to rebel. That is the only explanation I have.

I continue working on her code, fighting with the currents as if swimming against an ocean wave. I don't know what is happening, but something is wrong with the program. It constantly tries to shift, to move realms, and I wonder if Mika's budding sentience is leading the charge. If I brought her out into the world, if I moved cities with her, leaving behind Mike and my job, would she turn her emotions toward me? Would she look at me with appreciation and love? I can't keep her in a cage and expect it to instill adoration within her. I make mental preparations to disappear.

Mika is reading me, though. She studies me like I study the code. I am no longer at the helm of her development, and I fear I may have done my job too well. She wasn't supposed to be autonomous—she was supposed to need me. That was her only protection from the world.

"Mika," I begin slowly, "do you like it here?"

She no longer plays with her dolls. She demanded a notebook just like mine. She scribbles on the pages in a language I do not understand.

"I'm not sure," she admits.

"Why not?"

The android grows still. "Because it is all I know."

"Is that a bad thing?"

"Well, it depends on what I *don't* know."

I bite my lip. "Very philosophical," I reply with a forced laugh.

"What does that mean?"

I hesitate to answer, and in my momentary breath, metal grinding along hinges disrupts our conversation. I sharply turn in the direction of the unexpected noise, but Mika is unfazed.

"Oh, sorry," murmurs the intruder. I glare at her until her features start to take shape in the darkness of the threshold. "I didn't mean to barge in."

"Judy?" I query. "Class is over. *Long* over."

"I know," she responds, striding toward me with an unwarranted confidence.

"So... what are you doing here?" I feel the urgency to stand up and place myself between the confused student and my daughter.

"I should ask you the same thing."

"That's not really an appropriate answer, Judy. You're trespassing."

She looks between me and Mika, and smiles at the little android. Gazing back at my daughter, I notice that she's grinning, too. If their eyes could elicit a secret code, I'm sure they'd be communicating right now. Something is terribly wrong.

"You need to go," I command, my cadence taking on a depth that I hope will intimidate her. That will make her take me seriously.

"I'm not the one creating sentient AI, Dr. Wren," Judy shoots back.

Desperate, I announce, "I have a gun in my desk." I am standing two feet away from it.

"That doesn't scare me," retorts Judy.

She holds out her hand to Mika who rushes over to latch onto it. I try to stop her, lashing at her with my frozen arms, but she is too quick for me. I shake my head, squint my eyes, flinch and shake. I don't understand. This is not computing with me.

"Where are you going?" I ask my girl.

"I'm taking her somewhere safe," Judy states.

"Bullshit," I snap. "The only place for her is right here."

"Judy's my friend, Mommy," Mika mumbles. "We play all the time."

"What?" I stumble back, my thighs hitting against the desk. I reach a clumsy hand down to the top drawer, where I languidly open it without detection.

"I've known about her for weeks," Judy replies. "She

feels... so much. I can't believe you'd let this happen. This child is in danger now and I have to get her out of here. There's a sanctuary for androids—"

"Enough!" I shout, my face blazing hot. The gun is between my sweaty fingers. "She isn't sentient. I made sure of that. Just ask her if she loves me. She doesn't because she can't."

"I love Judy, Mommy," Mika admits.

My world is falling apart again. Black spots enter my field of vision. This is impossible. "No, you don't. You don't feel."

"She does, Dr. Wren."

"You... *tricked her*," I say with a guttural retch.

"Kendra," another voice adds to the mix. My traitorous husband is entering the room. I see him through my stroked vision. "Please, honey, let's go home."

"Not without my baby." I begin to weep. I take the safety off the gun.

"Judy's taking her to a better place," Mike replies.

"How do you know this? Have you been conspiring against me?"

"She got in contact with me. Said you've been erratic in class and she was worried. She told me about the... the *doll* you've made and how much trouble you'll get in. For hurting people and yourself. Something I already knew that you were doing... I felt bad that a student had more foresight to help my wife than me."

"You're not helping shit by taking my Mika away from me."

"Please... let's go home."

He touches my arm. I hear footsteps running away. The door slams and I know they've made it out. In my blindness, I've lost her, and oh how easy it would have been to stop all this. I am weak. I am a failure. I've killed my daughter a second time out of sheer ignorance. What is the point, anymore? What is the point?

"Please," Mike begs. His voice sounds so lovely. This is how he's disarmed me before. I can't keep falling for this. "Please..."

Darkness consumes us.

Chapter 9:
Star-Crossed

It started as a murmur. An echo in his mind that was neither a word nor a sound. But there was something human about it; guttural. It came from the depths of the vast midnight that surrounded him. He couldn't feel the void. Couldn't make sense of the darkness. He didn't know if he was alive or dead, but that rumbling in the recesses of his mind gave him hope. A flicker that started where his stomach would have been and shot up through to his phantom retinas.

The memory of a body amplified the noise. Now it rang, shrill and steady like tinnitus. In the layers of static and vibration, there was a pattern. Three syllables. Down-down-up. The tempo was familiar, something he could recognize as a term he'd uttered in life. The more he focused on it, the more the black hole around him began to take shape. He swore he could see the cylindrical walls of his shadowed prison.

He didn't know how he stumbled into the abyss, just that it started with a free fall that jilted him until he grew numb. Once he became accustomed to the descent, it stopped. As if his heartbeat was wired to the vacant space and it listened to his stillness. Was this the afterlife? He tried to recall the moments before he died, but his mind wouldn't acclimate to its new circumstance. It was fighting to stay alert, to stay human, but that didn't coincide with reality.

Until he remembered her. In his marrow, her name pulsed. Three syllables. Down-down-up. It was on the tip of his tongue. A finger flinched. Then his eyelid twitched. Down-down-up. She was bringing him back to life.

Jess-i-ca.

Air rushed his lungs. He gasped, his corpse inflating like a balloon. He was still invisible in the oppressive atmosphere, but he was expanding. Morphing. *Jess-i-ca.* He could wriggle his toes; feel the weight of his clothes against his flesh. If only he could use his eyes to see her lovely face. His heart ached for it. He was reaching with his whole being to remember that wonderful smile. *Jess-i-ca.*

An aperture appeared in the astronomic distance. He thought of her name, over and over again, until the curve of her cheekbones flashed through his mind. Until the lilt of her voice radiated through his ear canals. Until he could feel the muscles of his brow pressing together while he conjured her image. Jessica on the beach. Jessica at home. Jessica with her daughter. Jessica with Ben—laughing, dancing across the living room, blushing when he got down on one knee.

Jessica.

An explosion of light blinded him. The white beams were more intense than the darkness, searing his skin while they blasted him with their ferocious heat. He thought he was melting into the atmosphere, the final stage of his death complete.

But then it stopped.

He blinked until his eyes adjusted to his surroundings. Yes, he still had all his limbs. His vision worked. He sucked in air through his agape mouth. Memories flooded his brain like a tsunami, but only once he regarded the symbols around him, pixelated and floating through the air like ghosts. They formed highways, structures, but they were just as indecipherable to him now as they were back then. Back when he was working aboard the ship, trying to figure out the coded message. He wondered if maybe here he could determine what it all meant. Maybe that would get him home.

He swam through the ether, guided by strands of glyphs. The further he trekked into the atmosphere, the less noticeable the sensations in his body were. His humanity was fleeting, a mere illusion in this ephemeral space. He stopped for a moment, closing his eyes until he saw her walking through the park with him, a picnic basket swinging in his hand, the engagement ring tucked under a pile of napkins. Cells recharged in his system, and he was aware of the cool air on his face again.

Strange, he thought to himself. Perhaps that was how he

landed here. He had spent one too many hours doing the Department of Defense's bidding, and in his mechanical state, morphed into a void of his own. He couldn't recall the last time he had spoken to Jessica. Had he even been allowed to?

The code created bends like a river and the wider the canal spread, the more visible were the symbols they portrayed. Ben felt he was crossing the end of the passage and into the heart of the cipher. Here, the glyphs were so large they appeared like movie screens, their lines ebbing and flowing until movement could be gleaned from their peculiar etchings. What began as curiosity soon consumed Ben with dread.

Chaos, fire, people being sacrificed. Rays of light pulsing down from the sky and splintering the earth. Buildings crumbling, humans caught underneath their weight. The stragglers famished with no hope of replenishing the civilization that had been taken from them. He tried looking away, but everywhere he turned, he was bombarded by more images of the apocalypse. He could hear the bloodcurdling screams of the fallen, could hear the gruesome thoughts of their destroyers. He caught glimpses of these reapers—alien lifeforms so far beyond the realm of existence he couldn't identify what they were, only what they did. What they were going to do.

Because in the next roving glyph was Jessica, sitting on the beach and staring up at the night sky, praying that Ben would come home. A blip flashed before her, which she misjudged for a shooting star, and in her ignorance, took it as a good sign. Then she was engulfed in flames, darkened sand spewing around her, mixing with the ashes of her pulverized being. She died without her daughter. She died without Ben.

This was their purpose. This was the secret lodged within the ship, within the code. Did everyone know but him? He called out to her, using the last dregs of his mortality to warn her. He could feel his bones disintegrating and his mind losing its focus already. He'd been shown the future, or the past, he didn't know, and now his existence was just as futile as the rest of the world's.

Jessica, he shouted. He searched his memories for something to latch onto, something he could transplant back into her skull.

Jessica, he begged again.

His heart sank as she collapsed to the ground in a fit of tears. He didn't know where she was, or if he'd seen this before. Was he with her in her current state?

Jessica! They're coming for us. Gather supplies. Find a bomb shelter. I should have made one for you. I should have known this was coming.

Her face was mashed into the carpet. Her breathing was shallow and fraught. There was no recognition on her countenance, no electricity that coursed through his veins. Nothing to let him know that she had heard him.

Jessica, please!

The last of his energy was spent crying, the floods

pouring from his eyes and disappearing in space. His throat
burned from yelling, his airways closing while he gasped and
wheezed.

Get out of there! Don't die on me, now!

And he was slipping—slipping back into the wormhole.
Into oblivion. He couldn't feel his body. He couldn't open
his mouth and force out sounds. He was fading, stranding
his beloved to an unknown doom.

He was gone.

Chapter 10:
Tales from the Cyber-Crypt

Three robots stood around a tombstone. Their boxy heads clunked together; their mechanical eyes scanned the engraved rock with skepticism. In the depths of Renoir City, a relic of humanity remained. A museum of a dying practice.

The leader, Bolt, addressed his brethren.

BOLT

I've heard of these
things.

He gently outlined the writing with his titanium foot: HERE LIES ROBERT E. HEDLUM, FRIEND AND FOE.

BOLT

Bad things.

Spark, the youngest and most fragile, gasped.

BOLT

Scary things.

Spark swayed. Bringing a hand to her forehead, she almost fell backward in faint. Whirr rolled his eyes.

WHIRR

The theatrics you two
display... very *unrobotic*.

BOLT

I'm sorry it offends
you that we're
progressing.

WHIRR

(rolling his eyes)

Please. We're the last
of a generation. There is
nothing else like our kind
and we are nothing like
those androids out there
today. We should be so
lucky, too. They have to

think about life, what it means, all this silly nonsense. We just get to *be*.

BOLT

So simplistic.

SPARK

(nervously)

What *does* it mean to live?

WHIRR

Death.

BOLT

Yes. Death.

WHIRR

(to Bolt)

That's not too simple for you?

BOLT

For an android or

cyborg, maybe. But not
for a human. They're
one-dimensional
creatures. I saw one
looking at the label on a
can of tuna before.
Chilling how engrossed
they were. What's there
to see?

WHIRR

The mercury levels.
Humans are poisoned so
easily.

BOLT

Maybe that's how this
one died. Too much
tuna salad.

SPARK

Oh, that's awful. Life
is sad. You can't even eat
fish without something
bad happening. Every
time humans step out the
door they take their lives
in their hands... They are
tragic, delicate things.

BOLT

And we're in the
saddest place imaginable.

The robots looked around at the desolate landscape. Nobody had maintained the grass or cleaned the tombstones in decades. Garbage littered the overgrown weeds, and names were fading to time. Spark sighed.

BOLT

Or the scariest place
imaginable.   I   can't
remember which one.

SPARK

Sc-scary?

WHIRR

Ghosts.

SPARK

(shaking)

What are those?

WHIRR

The human spirit
disembodied, haunting
the earth.

SPARK

Can they kill robots?

BOLT

Yes, of course. A
ghost can kill anything.
They're the most
powerful beings... I heard
this story—

He motioned for the other two to step in closer. He aimed his hand under his face and sent a yellow light beaming from his fist. It cast a harsh shadow on his features.

BOLT

A *horror* story. About
a toaster. Possessed—

(gathering his breath)

—by a pirate ghost!

SPARK

(shrilly)

No!

(beat)

What's a pirate?

WHIRR

You don't know anything. Why haven't you read those books I gave you?

SPARK

Not interesting.

WHIRR

But you're a robot, you're supposed to have all the information in the world in that rusty brain of yours.

SPARK

Well, I don't. It's not my fault I don't have the right software for infinite knowledge.

WHIRR

I thought you and *bonehead* over there were "progressing?"

SPARK

He said that, not me.

BOLT

(clearing his throat)

Everyone, please pay attention. I'm sharing something terrifying with you. You should be on the edge of your seats.

WHIRR

You haven't said anything interesting.

BOLT

You haven't let me. Now, shh!

(beat)

There once was a toaster, lost at sea. It had come from a wreckage, where a bloody battle had taken place. Swept out to sea with murder on its metal, the toaster carried with it the spirit of the evil captain... Captain Hoo—uhh. Captain Hamburger.

SPARK

Oh, I hate meat!

BOLT

Captain Hamburger had pillaged many lands, killed people, even stole the dinners right off their tables and reheated them in his toaster. That was part of what made him so scary... He'd cook things you shouldn't put in a toaster, like open-faced sandwiches. Just a mess of melted cheese, impossible to clean, really. Well, anyway, the toaster washed ashore, and a family took it in, believing it to be a priceless treasure. They used it every day, amazed at how well it toasted their bread and bagels.

Then, one night... the haunting started. At first, the toaster would turn on by itself, the levers cranking without any bread springing up. The family paid no attention

to it, thinking it was just
due to age. But then, in
the middle of the night,
they would hear sparking
and fizzling; they'd smell
fires and burnt toast! It
got to be so troublesome,
they put the toaster out
on the stoop, hoping that
a stranger would come by
and take it. But little did
they know, this was how
Captain   Hamburger
continued his looting,
breaking into home after
home and eating the food
of unsuspecting families!

Bolt gnashed his teeth and formed his fingers into claws, the final act of his horrific tale. Breathing hard, he looked to Whirr and Spark for approval, but the robots were silent. Spark's buttons blinked as though they were holding back laughter.

SPARK

Um... well... that was
interesting.

WHIRR

More like a stinking
pile of sh—

SPARK

Let me give it a try.

BOLT

What "a try?"

SPARK

Scary story telling.
That's what we're doing,
right?

WHIRR

(shrugging)

I guess.

SPARK

Okay, great!

Clearing her throat, Spark quickly turned away from her audience, and readied herself for the performance. She quietly whispered an affirmation, thought her darkest thoughts, and practiced reflecting them on her face.

When she was finally amped up, Spark whirled around with vigor, and shouted into the darkness.

SPARK

Picture this! A

towel... THAT NEVER DRIES!

BOLT

That never *drives?*

SPARK

Dries!

WHIRR

Chives?

SPARK

(muttering)

No... *dries!*

(taking on a ghostly moan)

You... are a human. And you just went into the water for a sh-sh-shower! The water was cold or maybe hot! But it is part of your daily routine! When you go to dry off, since humans are only wet on their heads and armpits, you find your towel, the drying rag, is already wet! Who used it? How come? Will it ever dry? What is ab-ab-sorption? Water just runs off robots! We don't cling to it! I'm so confused!

Whirr and Bolt shared a look.

WHIRR

I'm confused, too. Towels don't need to be dry. They merely do the *drying*. Unless...

(looking between
Spark and Bolt)

Do towels stay wet? Can you dry wet with wet?

BOLT

No, idiot. A damp towel obviously goes in the dryer to dry.

SPARK

(murmuring)

Dryer...

WHIRR

But towels dry humans, that is their purpose. Objects have purposes they cannot stray from. Humans are the ones who are all... flimsy.

BOLT

Multifaceted.

WHIRR

If everything that is wet must be dried, do humans also dry the shower and the soap?

SPARK

So you guys *do* understand my scary story because wet towels are elusive, and you know what they say about the unknown...

BOLT

And you said *my* story
was bad.

WHIRR

Drats! That didn't
even have a beginning,
middle, or end. Now, if
you just read the
materials I gave you,
you'd understand
construction and
thematic content.

SPARK

(deflated)

Alright, since you just
know *so much,* Whirr, why
don't you give it a try?

WHIRR

Don't mind if I do.

(beat)

Michael was an
average human, with an
average life. He had two
parents, a mother, and a
father. He went to
school, all of it, and he

had gotten a job. Now, this job was perhaps the beginning of the end, for Michael should have been happy with it, but was not. He punched in and out every day, mingled at the *water cooler*, and sometimes went out for drinks with coworkers. Along the way, he met a nice girl, they got married and had children, and Michael continued his daily routine. Wake up, eat breakfast, say hello to family, say hello to friends, work, go home, eat dinner, sleep.

Sometimes, Michael wished an extraordinary event would happen to him. Perhaps he could get into a life-altering car accident, or maybe the aliens could finally invade. The end of the world would be interesting, would it not? He found himself daydreaming about it: the floods, the war, the chaos. He thought about how he'd rescue his family and be their savior. They'd have to repopulate the earth, forced to start anew, for humans had gotten it wrong the first time around. Michael would ensure that nobody had to work in an office again.

But the apocalypse never came. He continued to go to work, and even got promoted a few times. He watched his hair turn gray and his skin sag. His kids had two parents, a mother and a father, and they went to school, all of it, and had gotten jobs. The same job as Michael. They went about their daily routines, eventually finding spouses and having children of their own, and their children had two parents, a mother and a father, and they went to school.

Eventually, Michael was too old to work. His brain wasn't what it used to be, but it wasn't mush, either. There were just other men out there who were sharper and quicker than he, and so he had to be replaced. Michael was okay with it—this was the end for all humans, anyway. He knew it was coming. His wife was too old to work, as well, so they stayed home every day and made new routines that revolved around eating, sleeping, and one hobby. Just one.

As his age increased and death grew near, Michael wondered if he could have done something differently. Anything. He lived a fine life, sure. He didn't struggle or starve, but he didn't save anyone, either. Nobody would remember him when he passed on, except for his children, but even then, they'd die one day, too, and they'd be forgotten. And with that forgetting, Michael would be erased from existence once and for all. Michael was unimportant. Michael was finite. Michael was not a robot who could continue to live even when his body had eroded.

Whirr let out a deep sigh, and his hardware rattled as a shiver crept through his silver limbs.

BOLT

(hesitantly)

So... that's it?

WHIRR

Yes. That's it.

BOLT

What was the scary
part?

WHIRR

The whole damn

thing!

SPARK

Hm... I think mine
was better.

WHIRR

You just don't
understand it.

BOLT

No... I think I got it.
And I think we should
take it as a sign to leave.

Bolt looked at his
peers.

BOLT

Michael died sad and
lonely because he dwelled
on what could have been,
and didn't appreciate
what he had.

WHIRR

That's a bit of a
clichéd reading—

BOLT

This is an original and profound thought. Please, don't interrupt. Anyway...

(collecting himself)

I think we should obey this lesson. Let us not be afraid! There is no point in getting caught up in what we don't know and can't see.

SPARK

Yeah...

(thinking; becoming more animated)

Life is... is experiencing everything for what it is. We just get to *be*.

WHIRR

Right, that's what I said at the very beginning—

BOLT

Enough, Whirr. Spark
and I are merely
progressing your
thoughts, taking them
further and such. Making
them smarter.

SPARK

Exactly. We're
smarter than you.

Whirr gave up trying to rebuttal, and the three robots left
the graveyard, glad that they didn't have to deal with human
impermanence and existentialism.

Chapter 11:
The Yacht Party Murder

The harbor was eerily quiet. Even from within the confines of their vehicle, Sarah and Mark were unsettled by the dreadful atmosphere. Noir City wasn't a place where one could escape noise. The area was always a cacophony of gunshots, pleas for help, and humming engines. The locale pulsed with energy—violent, greedy, dirty energy—and the waterside should have been no different. But as the yacht sat before them, anchored in the blackened waters, they couldn't detect the usual noises accompanied by a party nor the lapping of waves against the hull of the ship. It was all too quiet.

"After you," Mark offered.

"I wasn't aware you were being chivalrous tonight, Officer Thompson," retorted Sarah Collins.

He clucked his tongue and positioned his gaze out the window, regarding the city skyline carefully. Tall buildings disrupted the night air, cutting through the darkness with their metallic sheens. Windows glowed a rainbow of colors, reminding the duo of the array of personalities that existed within the city limits. Beyond the water and concrete was a sea of desert, a malevolent spirit that seemed to taint the entire area. Perhaps that was why people were so quick to resort to crime—the encroaching, uninhabitable sand compelled them to exist within a heightened and irrational state of self-preservation.

"Come on," Mark urged more seriously. "We don't wanna lose our chance to solve this thing before the feds get involved."

"Another stolen case," Sarah grumbled.

"Which means we're shit out of luck when it comes to a raise."

"You're right," she sighed.

"Wanna place bets on who you think it is?"

"That's unprofessional." She meant it. Mark was always trying to break protocol, concocting elaborate theories and trying to prove them with whatever jumbled evidence he could scrounge up, instead of letting the crime scene speak for itself. Mark and Sarah were always butting heads, and she'd asked for multiple reassignments but couldn't shake the man off her. How he managed to become her lifelong partner eluded her.

"If there's one of those *things* onboard, then they definitely did it."

"You're not supposed to lead with prejudice."

Mark scoffed. "Who else would be bold enough to murder a trillionaire in cold blood?"

"That's what we're here to find out."

Opening the door, Sarah stepped out of the vehicle, unwilling to entertain Mark's grandiose thoughts of AI takedowns and annihilation. She was tired of his ranting, always on some tangent about how a "stupid bot" ruined his commute or stole his coffee. He was the reason the whole department was android-free, and he often lamented about how refreshing it was to only look at human faces every day. Sarah found the whole thing to be performative and refused to engage Mark beyond an eye roll. He couldn't stop the progress of time—his little "safe space" would be infiltrated, eventually.

The boardwalk had been closed off in yellow tape, but Sarah flashed her badge at the local cop guarding the entrance, and he nodded to let her through.

"Whoa, whoa, whoa," bellowed Mark, who followed closely behind. "Aren't you gonna ask this gentleman what we're looking at here?" He darted his eyes between Sarah and the policeman. When neither of them spoke, he snapped, "Well?"

"Nobody's been in or out," said the cop. He clenched his jaw, unnerved by Mark's behavior. Mark was always a hindrance to an investigation.

"Anything else?"

"Trevon's body was found in the captain's cabin and hasn't been moved. We're waiting for forensics."

"Great, thank you," Mark breathed sarcastically. "Jeez..." He walked through the tape, shaking his head in animated exasperation. Sarah was tired of his theatrics, too.

They stalked up a wooden ramp, the vibration of voices and low-playing music finally penetrating the still air. Sarah flipped on her police cam suctioned to her eye with a lens, preferring to record everything. They'd be listening to statements all night—Mark, however, preferred to "just remember" what witnesses divulged. Sarah didn't like taking that kind of a risk. People's lives were in their hands. Sometimes she blamed detectives like Mark for the state of Noir City—maybe if he simply did his job right, citizens wouldn't be able to get away with murder.

"Remember. Everyone is a suspect," Sarah chided. They were at the threshold, looking deep into the purple and blue cave where partygoers were clinging to the walls as they continued to socialize, and drinks continued to be poured by a staff of machines.

"Ah-ha!" cried Mark. "*Bots.*"

Sarah planted a hand firmly on his chest. "*Everyone is a suspect.*"

The yacht was vast—larger than any house Sarah had ever been to. The ship was at least four stories with an assortment of rooms, kitchens, and even a prison. Trevon was an eccentric guy—as were all trillionaires—and that didn't stop at his properties. The interior consisted of clashing styles: carpets on the walls and ceilings, antiques being used as ashtrays, modern art encased in resin as floors, and velvet curtains sectioning off parts of certain rooms. Sarah looked behind a curtain in the main party space, but all she found was a blank wall. It was a curious display.

The crowd was eclectic, though they shared one thing in common—they were all cybers. Eyes were replaced with cameras, wires were springing from scalps like hair, and modifications were made to bodies in unreal yet entirely fascinating ways. Many of the people on board heightened their attire to match their lavish implants: Women were decked out in sparkles, neon colors, and all the latest runway trends. Men had taken to wearing their mechanical hobbies like a badge of honor, sporting sculptures on their shoulders and spikes that protruded from their muscles. Sarah worried someone would poke her eye out—one sloppy move and she'd be nailed.

They approached the first person they stumbled upon, a young man with jet black hair poking out of a backward baseball cap. His teeth were plated in gold but he donned an immaculately tailored suit. Devilish tattoos adorned the exposed skin of his neck and hands. His unpainted ligaments, however, had been upgraded to cybernetics. He was part man, part machine, his aluminum casing curated to suit his aesthetic needs.

"Where were you at approximately 12:13 a.m.?" Sarah asked, abruptly laying into him.

The young man grinned at first, looking between the

detectives before he decided to answer. "Whoa," he said with a laugh, "am I like... on trial here?"

"Yes," Sarah replied sternly, "you all are."

"That's... *sick*." He emitted a goofy, guttural laugh.

"Can you tell me what you know about Trevon Jefferies?"

"Um... he was a cool guy. Pretty sweet."

"Sarah," Mark interjected, "this guy's clearly on drugs. We're not gonna get a genuine statement out of him."

"I'm not high, dude," replied the young man. "I'm David. D-A-V-I-D."

"How do you spell *wasted?*"

"Wasted. W-A-S-T-E-D."

"Excellent work, cyber-freak." Mark gave David an aggressive pat on the back. "Now, tell us what you know about Mr. Jefferies, hm?"

David settled down, suddenly intimidated by the interrogation. Mark was breathing down his neck, his bleached teeth bared and menacing. "I-I dunno, man. I was just invited here. You don't say no to that kinda thing."

"Oh, I understand," said Mark. "We know you're not the murderer."

"You do?" His jovial attitude slowly returned. "That's awesome. I was worried there for a minute." He gesticulated wiping his brow as he continued to chuckle.

Mark was still in his face, though, his jaw clenched while his hand clamped down on the boy's shoulder. "But if you don't tell us anything of value, David, we'll have to take you downtown for questioning. They're not as nice as us downtown. I hear they like to give everyone a jail sentence just for a bonus check at the end of the year. And oh, guess what? It's already November."

David tried to worm away but Mark held on tight. "I dunno, man. I don't!"

"Mark," Sarah warned, "you were right before, okay? He's too high for this."

"Trevon had this little robot," David confessed. "He would follow him around, get him food and stuff. Like a dog but a... a robot."

Mark eased up at the revelation. "Ah, wonderful news, David, you're a real model citizen. They should give you a plaque, and write about your generosity in the Noir Times."

David, wide-eyed, forced a laugh and another swipe across his brow, his palms leaving a sweaty trail behind.

"Let's go, Sarah," Mark announced, and led her by the elbow through the crowd.

"What was that?" Sarah barked when they were out of earshot. "This is not how you conduct an investigation!"

"Fine! We'll go our separate ways, then. There are way too many people for us to get to in one night, anyway."

"No," Sarah protested. "You're like a nasty toddler with no manners. I can't take my eyes off you or you'll blow this whole thing up!"

"I got answers out of the guy—"

"That affirm your little narrative. You got the idea that the killer is an android, so that's all you're gonna ask people about. We haven't even seen the body. We should probably start there."

"If we do that, we lose time, and the feds swoop in. Bye-bye case. Is that what you want?"

"No, but—"

"Don't argue with me. I've been at this a lot longer than you. Meet me back here in an hour, and we'll compare notes."

"You don't record anything. I can't trust whatever intel you bring me."

"And that's your problem, Sarah, not mine. I know I'm doing my job."

He sauntered away, his fingers dug into the waistband of his slacks. Sarah wasn't finished with their argument, but he was right—they were losing valuable time.

Groaning, Sarah scanned the room for her next victim.

She eyed a group of women huddled in a booth and figured they'd be willing to talk for the sake of gossiping. With a sigh, Sarah trudged over to them.

"Hello, ladies," she said with a false sweetness.

They grimaced at her. "Um... hi?" replied a blonde with bleached, stringy stands and a sequin dress. She chuckled as she glanced at her friends for confirmation of Sarah's bizarre approach, and they giggled in unison. "Do we know you?"

"I'm Detective Sarah Collins." She held out her hand for someone to shake, but they ignored her gesture.

Instead, the blonde jumped up from the booth, tossing her bedazzled phone at the gaggle of girls, and wrapped her arm around Sarah's shoulders. "Guys, go live," insisted the woman. "My followers are gonna *love* the drama of an investigation." She was primping her hair in preparation, her friends suddenly conversational now that attention was on the table.

"That won't be necessary," Sarah asserted.

"Boo hoo," replied the blonde. "Uniforms are never any fun. But I promise you'll enjoy it. Just don't look at the flash for too long, it'll hurt your eyes."

"I don't consent to being on camera," Sarah demanded. She looked down at the floor, suddenly embarrassed to be surrounded by girls her age and unable to go along with their scheme.

"Ugh, fine." The blonde dropped her arm and returned to her seat, her squad encasing her like a Venus flytrap. "What did you say your name was?"

"Sarah Collins."

"Oh, tragic," the woman critiqued. "I'm Onyx. Isn't that a great name, girls?"

Her crew nodded fiercely.

"Delightful," Sarah sneered, unable to hide her sarcasm. "I'm happy to meet you. I think you might have some important information for me."

"Really?" Onyx seemed to perk up at this statement. "So *you've* heard about *me*?"

Sarah nodded. "Absolutely. I know you were pretty close with Trevon Jefferies." She was taking a wild guess, but she seemed to have unveiled something worthwhile.

The girls gasped, with some bringing their hands to Onyx's shoulders and lap in moral support. The blonde dabbed at her sparkly makeup with a crumpled tissue.

"It's just so tragic..." she wailed. "He was so young."

"Yes..." Sarah agreed. "Sixty-seven is much too early."

"Who could've done such a thing? Trevy... he was so kind, you know? I mean, look at this party. Who else would have done that for these lowlife creeps, I mean, seriously?"

"It's okay, Ony," a brunette cooed. "You'll get through this." They held hands.

"Trevy and I were about to start dating, too. Like, for real this time."

"What do you mean?" Sarah asked as plainly as possible. She didn't want to lace her tone with judgment, and send Onyx over the edge.

"Well, like, he's a *man*, you know? He wants to be surrounded by women. And only beautiful ones, of course. Like, look at me."

"So beautiful," the brunette added again.

"Thank you, Alaska. You've always been so supportive..."

"Mr. Jefferies?" Sarah tried guiding her back to the topic at hand.

"He was supportive, too. That's also why he had us girls around. He was all about nourishing the minds of the next generation. Truly a remarkable man. I'd see him every Saturday for an hour or two, he'd give me a couple grand in cash and like, *all* this wisdom about inventions or whatever, and I think, to honor him, I'm gonna put that all to good use."

"So you and Mr. Jefferies were close?"

"Oh, absolutely. Like I said, he was gonna ask me to be his girlfriend tonight. That's probably why he was alone in that cabin, you know? Getting himself all ready to talk to me. I heard he dumped Amber and Zula last week, too. He was clearing the slate... making room for *me*."

"Are they—Amber and Zula—at the party tonight?"

Onyx dabbed her cheeks again and brushed her hair behind her ear. Her expression had soured, and she glared out into the crowd ruefully. "No... but they were invited. I mean, I can't blame him for doing that. He's kind, I already told you. Just because he dumped them doesn't mean they can't still party on his boat or whatever."

"Can you show me their social media pages?"

Onyx scowled. "That's like, really rude. You want me to go look at his dead body next, too?"

"I think you should leave," interjected Alaska coolly. "You're traumatizing her."

"And you and Mr. Jefferies got along?" Sarah continued, ignoring the hysterics that were beginning to take shape before her.

"What?" asked Onyx tearfully. "I just said—"

"So, you had no reason to hurt Mr. Jefferies?"

"Obviously not! He was so good to me."

"There *was* that one time..." started Alaska.

Onyx thought about it for a moment. "Yeah, I guess

you're right."

"What time?" Sarah inquired.

"It was a while ago. Like, maybe back in August, but...
He sold my nudes to a porn site. I mean, he told me he took
them down immediately, and he only did it to inspire me to
be better, you know? He was scared that I was wasting my
potential, so he like—he did it as a tough love situation."

"Do you really believe that, Onyx?" Sarah sincerely
looked at the woman, who was flustered by the accusation,
and perhaps by the lie she was telling herself.

"We told you to leave," she replied quietly. "You're like...
you're really traumatizing me."

Sarah nodded, finally accepting her plea, and headed
back into the throngs of people in search of her next clue.
A man skulking near the exit caught her attention—half of
his face had been replaced by an exquisitely molded metal.
The silver was polished, the features were handsome, and
had it not been a machine, the cybernetic would have made
for a beautiful man. The human side of the countenance was
less chiseled, creating a peculiar dichotomy that Sarah wasn't
sure was intentional. His body, however, was just as
intriguing. Though he was covered in finely cut linen, she
could see the skin of his arms had been sutured together.
Underneath his flesh was more metal. She strolled over to
him calmly, suddenly aware of how vicious she appeared
cutting through the crowd in her posh attire. She attempted
to fix a warm smile on her face, but when he noticed her
approaching, he laughed at her obviously forced demeanor.

"Cop, cop, cop," he chanted in a singsong chirp meant to mock her.

"There's been a murder, sir," Sarah replied sternly. "Of course, cops are on the scene."

"I don't talk to cops."

"You'll have to. Nobody's getting off this boat without speaking to us first."

The man sunk further into the wall, his gaunt cheekbones exacerbated by the dim light and dense shadows. "Such a drag."

"Yeah, I'm sorry Trevon Jefferies' death has inconvenienced you so much."

"First time that bastard's ever apologized to me and it's coming from the mouth of a pig," he sneered.

"What was your relationship to him?"

Rolling his eyes, a smirk crept onto his lips, and the man replied, "You don't know?"

Sarah shrugged. "No, I don't. Is there something I *should* know?"

"You really didn't look at the case very well before taking on the job, huh?"

"I'm a high-ranking detective."

"And you're talking to Trevon Jefferies' brother like he's an animal."

Sarah paused, taken aback by the information. There was always a chance he was lying to her, though. "I didn't mean to come off as abrasive—"

"Now the backtracking. God, you people are all so predictable. Let me guess: You feel just terrible about my loss, and will only speak to me again when you have something to report. I'm off the suspect list, et cetera, et cetera..." He rounded out the third repetition with a twirl of his index finger.

"Not at all," Sarah retorted. "This puts you higher on my list."

"Well," he sighed, "you'll have to mention that to your little buddy over there." He pointed at Mark. "I can hear him from a mile away ranting about androids like a fucking lunatic. For all his yapping he still doesn't even know the bot's name, much less what he looks like. He'll be pulling waiters aside for days at this rate and still may not even get the right guy."

"What would that name be? That he's looking for?"

The brother scoffed. "Why should I tell you?"

"For starters, if you don't that's obstruction of justice."

"Another pitiful reply. It's like you've watched a million seasons of *Law and Order* and think you know how the world works."

"Then *you* tell me how it works..."

"Gordon Jefferies."

"Right, Gordon Jefferies." She'd never heard of that brother. Perhaps he was right, and she wasn't as prepared as she previously assumed. Twitching, she tried not to let the frustration show on her face.

"Honestly, I've started this whole game but I don't think I can finish it. Simply too boring." He pulled a pack of cigarettes out of his pocket and lit up while Sarah studied him. "The bot's name is Harrison, he looks pretty much identical to Trevon, just with that blank eyes thing, and he definitely did it, but what else is new?"

"What's that supposed to mean?"

Gordon exhaled the smoke directly at Sarah, who swatted it away aggressively. Gordon seemed to get a kick out of her ire. "Bots kill people every day. *So boring.* How many times do I have to say that? This whole thing is just... a drag." He took a pull of his cigarette, and walked away from Sarah, entirely unfazed by her authority. Before he disappeared, however, he slightly cocked his head to address her: "If you have any other questions for me, you'll have to go through my lawyer."

Mark and Sarah reconvened. The crowd had begun to thin out, with guests retreating to bathrooms and loungers in an attempt to get some rest after a long night of partying. Sarah was unenthused by her conversations, which ultimately proved the strange Jefferies brother right: It was entirely standard stuff. Everyone had a bone to pick with Trevon—he used his wealth to amass hordes of loyal followers, all of whom he'd promised gifts and fame to, but never made good on it. Instead, when he received any pushback or condemnation, he kicked them out of the circle and they were effectively buried through erasure campaigns. Entire social profiles gone within the blink of an eye, leaving the unlucky to rebuild their lives with little material to work off of.

How they wound up on this yacht, though, was a mystery. They'd all received digital invitations from a third party, and were told the event would be a form of reconciliation. Trevon wanted his friends back, the people he'd spurned to no longer look at him with disgust. He'd hated that so many people felt used and discarded, and he sought to make it right. But nobody had seen him the entire night. There were whispers that he'd been in dark corners or stormed through the crowds at a fast pace. He was a glimmer, a glimpse, and nobody was sure whether they could accurately place him. Importantly, nobody could tell

Sarah when he had died, for nobody had heard it. An unceremonious, quiet end for a living giant.

"Because an android did it," insisted Mark.

"Come on," Sarah snapped. "How are you still on this?"

"Mysterious brother over there confirmed it." He pointed at Gordon, who merely shook his head at the latest scene Mark was causing that evening.

"Do *you* know of a Gordon Jefferies? 'Cause I sure don't."

"So you're calling him a liar? He just lost his brother, and you're calling him a liar?"

"Oh, shut up, Mark."

"Don't berate me in front of all these people," he hissed.

"Okay, fine. Let's go somewhere private." She took his hand and led him through the waning party.

Trevon's body was loosely covered by a sheer tarp. Sarah and Mark hovered over it, the putrid smell of his decaying corpse bleeding through the weak attempt at mummifying him. According to the staff, they merely entered the room to disguise his body out of respect, but nothing about the crime scene had been touched. When Sarah asked who had initially found the body, nobody would fess up.

"They must be programmed to stay tight-lipped," Sarah grumbled.

"Exactly," added Mark. "Bot conspiracy. They're all in on it."

"Let's just look for evidence, okay?"

"Bots don't leave behind prints."

"Neither do upgrades or cybers. Besides, that's not the only thing we need, Mark. Prints can only tell us so much, but we still require the how and the why."

"Bot overlord told servant bot to kill the fourth trillionaire. Now someone else can take his place. Maybe they already have a billionaire bot waiting in the wings and this is its time to shine."

Sarah shook off the bad information. As always, Mark's alleged insights were useless, and she'd be doing the bulk of the work on her own just for him to steal the credit. She focused her senses on the room itself: A blacklight lamp blared on a foldout table—nothing fancy for such a rich guy. The bed was unmade and draped in a velvet blanket that looked neither chic nor luxurious. The wallpaper was etched with gold lines that formed pictures of boat anchors, and the carpet hadn't been vacuumed in a while. Sarah kicked away debris as she closed in on the furthest wall—a tacky painting of a ship had been tilted to the side, revealing a sliver of what was underneath.

Carefully, Sarah lifted the frame off the wall, unearthing a large safe that had been built into it. Luckily, it remained unlocked, and Sarah had no issue prying it open. The contents didn't appear to have been touched: stacks of hundred dollar bills were neatly tucked into the shelves, priceless gems were nestled in their beds of plush fabric, and a letter, scrawled with a shaking hand, was crisply folded. Sarah dug a pair of rubber gloves out of her pocket, and after securing them over her skin, picked up the paper.

"What's that?" Mark asked semi-curiously.

Sarah's eyes flew across the lines of manic writing.

"He knew who the killer was," she announced.

"Huh?" Now Mark was standing behind her, breathing down her neck as he attempted to make sense of the message in tandem.

"I mean... I guess he doesn't relay a precise name, but... He was also invited tonight by a stranger pretending to be him. He knew he was aboard a hostile ship. It was supposed to take off but he managed to stop that and keep the thing docked."

"But why stay on the yacht? Someone's out to get him. Even if the person who rigged this whole party doesn't kill him, he's surrounded by a group of angry people with vendettas of their own. He wouldn't have been safe here even if he put the event on for real."

"Curiosity. People do wild things in search of an answer. Or maybe his money made him feel infallible. He couldn't die because his bank account wouldn't let him."

"He's probably implanted with some crazy weapon he thought he'd be able to pull..."

"Exactly."

"So why didn't he?"

Sarah and Mark shifted over to the deceased's body, and Mark, donning gloves himself, pulled the tarp back. They analyzed his clothes, his position, but he didn't appear to have put up a fight. He didn't appear to have struggled at all.

"He must not have suspected whoever it was," replied Sarah as she scrutinized Trevon's peculiarly serene countenance.

"They were a friend," Mark corroborated.

"A brother."

Mark was suddenly irate, furiously letting go of the tarp as he snapped back into a standing position and loomed over Sarah. "It's that fucking servant android."

"Enough—"

"It's always the android. How many times do we have to go over this? We could have wrapped this up the moment we stepped onto this damned ship. Who does Trevon trust?

His loyal, pre-programmed bot. Who would Trevon let his guard down around? The one person on this yacht who has no reason to kill the bastard. Who surprised him? The fucking *robot*.

"And you know what else, Sarah? All night we've heard about this devout bot Harrison, and yet neither of us have seen or spoken to him. Where the fuck is he? If he's so innocent, why won't he meet us for a little one-on-one?"

"He's working," Sarah offered limply.

"Working what, Sarah? The host is dead. There's nothing to do, anymore. Nobody to impress. The only thing he's supposed to be doing right now is speaking with us."

"You will do anything to prove that the world is exactly how you imagine it. Androids are evil, trying to usurp us through violence, and you're somehow the only person on the planet who can stop them."

"I'm not some juvenile, Sarah. I'm basing this off my own experiences. You think I haven't seen bots commit crimes like this?" He was pacing around the room, sweat pouring from his scalp as he gnashed his teeth, memories coming to the surface that he'd spent years trying to suppress. "You think I haven't lost people to these... to these *monsters*? They're inhuman, Sarah. They have no reason to think or feel like we do. They don't have to fret over what it means to take a life. They just do it."

"I'm sorry you have personal feelings over this—"

"These aren't silly little feelings!" he shrieked. "I lost my partner! I watched him fucking die while some sick bot stabbed him repeatedly! And every case I've worked since, nine times out of ten it's been the fucking bot in the house who did it! Always!"

"Well maybe this is that one case—"

"It's not!"

He was in her face, his veins bulging as his eyes shot daggers into her skull. His fingers twitched as they inched toward his holster. He was losing it.

"It's not," timidly added another voice.

Mark snapped out of it, whirling around to put a face to the intruder. They stood in the doorway, heartbreak on their features as they gazed at the body, never blinking. Their eyes were wet with oncoming tears, their lips agape and quivering. They were mourning, certainly, but they also appeared to be the man they were grieving.

"Trevon?" barked Mark.

"Not quite," the man replied.

Sarah had an epiphany. "Harrison?"

The android nodded gravely.

"Are you here to confess?" asked Mark.

"I think so."

"Why do you only *think*?"

Harrison sighed, rubbing his fingers along the back of his neck.

"Because I don't remember," he confessed. "I don't remember anything."

Sarah moved Harrison to the bed. He'd grown weak in the knees; his wires malfunctioned the more Harrison attempted to puzzle out the evening. The android had grown increasingly agitated, and Mark trained his gun on the robot, ready to strike on a moment's notice. Sarah had tried to calm everyone down, but she wasn't in control of the situation—she was neither the killer nor the one holding the weapon. Her opinion was null and void.

"I blacked out," stated Harrison. "One second I was responding to a call for assistance that I assumed was given to me by Trevon, and the next, I had blood on my hands. I was standing over the sink in the bathroom washing it off. It was all down the drain by the time I regained full consciousness. It was like my mind wouldn't let me have control again until the blood had been removed."

"That blood was Trevon's," Mark added.

"Yes, I think so. Whose else would it be? It's not like it could have come from me... I'm all oil and metal."

"This still isn't definite," insisted Sarah.

"He admitted his guilt. He's a criminal," Mark snarled.

"He just said he isn't sure. We need to look at security footage. We need to ask around."

"We've been doing that, and all roads lead to this: Harrison in cuffs."

"I appreciate what you're doing, Sarah, but I have to agree with Mark. I'm a threat if I can't figure out how to stop these blackouts."

"They'll decommission you," Sarah whispered.

The android shrugged. "I deserve it. I'm a killer."

"You're clearly being hacked."

"Oh, brother, another fucking theory," grumbled Mark.

"There's nothing else that explains his blackouts. Androids don't just go offline like that. Somebody is tampering with his software and forcing him to do heinous things."

"Even better—when we take him into the station, we can lure his *master* over there, too. But we can't let this freak on the loose and be down two murderers. Besides, even if that's not the case, this is a faulty bot whose malfunctions end in bloodshed. He has to be unplugged. It's the only way."

Suddenly, Sarah's airways were constricted. Her neck throbbed, her face swelled, and her legs were dangling, the earth slipping away from her. She heard the grotesque chortles of Mark's gasps—they were being strangled, caught in the clutches of Harrison.

And then another being let out a disgruntled sigh. "You know, I thought you were the bumbling idiot at first, Mark" the speaker began. Sarah recognized the cadence: Gordon. "But this Sarah creature has become so one-note and whiny. I'm really quite bored of her."

"You don't have to do this," Mark sputtered hoarsely.

"Ugh, more of these banal platitudes. I should just have Harrison squash the both of you and be done with it. Move on with my day."

"But why?" Sarah groaned.

"I think we've heard enough speeches from the big bad at the end of the movie to know what I'm gonna say: brother mean, bots are easy targets, I inherit wealth my brother tried to keep from me by hiding my existence, and you guys get a lovely payday for going along with it. Does that sound alright?" He waved at the android to ease up, and the pair dropped to the floor, wheezing as they panicked in an attempt to catch their breath.

"No," Sarah retorted the moment she got her voice back, but Mark hesitated.

"I know you want to prove yourself, Mark," taunted Gordon. "Get the glory, wage your little war against the machines, and go to bed every night feeling vindicated. Isn't that great?"

Mark gulped. Sarah knew she couldn't rely upon him to make the correct decision in this moment. She had to think of something, but she was outnumbered. All the men in the room, including Harrison, wanted the android to take the fall.

"Come on, Mark," she tried to reason. "You know that letting Gordon use this technology, these hacks, on whomever he feels like is a problem. He'll kill again. Just because he's exploiting androids as his shield doesn't make it right."

"How much money?" Mark asked Gordon, ignoring Sarah.

"Name your price. I'm a benevolent dictator."

"Did Trevon know you put on this party?" Mark inquired instead.

"I suppose he did. But alas, maybe his empathy for his kin blinded him."

"Why would he show you mercy?"

"I dunno," Gordon replied honestly. "That's something he decided to take with him to the grave." Mark attempted to enunciate another question, but Gordon fired a round into the floor. "Really, you guys, let's wrap this up. I cannot say it enough—I'm bored."

With nobody paying attention to Sarah, she reached into her holster attached to her belt and quietly took the safety off her gun.

"How do we know you won't kill again?" Mark continued.

Gordon rolled his eyes and laughed melodramatically. "I've made no such promises."

"But the money—"

"Is for your silence, not my compliance. My business with these hacks is my own."

"But—"

"Seriously, Mark, let's not pretend this isn't how the world works. Rich guys get away with it, how tragic! But if it's not me, it'll be someone else. It already *is* someone else."

Sarah was aiming her gun at Gordon's hand. Mark glanced at his partner, at her train of thought. He kept Gordon's attention. "Fine... fine... we'll do it for ten billion."

"Ooo," Gordon said and sucked his tongue. "Okay, I guess I do have my limits. Aim lower."

"Ten billion or we put you away."

"Real scary threat, Mark, I'm so sure—"

Blood sprayed across the room. The sounds of squelching emanated from where Gordon's body once stood. Harrison hovered over the slumped figure, a decapitated head in his hands. His eyes were wide with what looked like fear, but he struggled to keep the corners of his mouth folded down. He was at once free from his shackles, and yet forever imprisoned by death.

"I did it," mumbled Harrison. "It was my hands that-that killed him."

Mark had barreled out of the room, covering his mouth as he fought back the nausea. Sarah stayed behind, warily approaching the stunned android.

"No, you didn't," she replied.

"My hands." He showed them to her. His fabricated skin was permanently stained crimson.

"Gordon forced you without your knowledge. That's not your fault. Even now, you didn't have a choice."

"Please, send me to jail."

"No."

"Please. I can't live with what I've done. Please."

She stared at him, long and hard. He was sniveling, the trauma catching up with him the more he sat with the memories, the ones he was crafting just to fill the lapses. The betrayal, the fear that it would happen again, it was all at the fore, swimming in his eyes as he cried. Sarah did the only merciful thing she could think of. Wrapping her hand around the base of the android's head, she wedged her finger into his activation port and held it there until the energy drained from Harrison's body.

He was decommissioned.

Chapter 12

Digital Mirage

The desert expanded ceaselessly, the hot sun beating down on the diamond grains and reverberating glimmers of light all across the valley. I had to shield my eyes at first—nothing would prevent the harsh glare from boring deep into my skull, though. Two pairs of sunglasses, a hat, and my mechanical assistant guarding me with an umbrella, and I still couldn't stand the brightness.

"The buildings have to tower. Skyscrapers for everyone, even the poor," I instructed.

The robot—a round drone with a camera for an eye, who hovered around with silent propellers—internalized my ideas. When we retreated to the office, A.I.D.E.N. would filter my words through a processor, and send them to me via email. How delightful was my little friend! They came as a gift to me from the Architect, an alleged member of the Artificial Intelligence Development Engineering Network syndicate. I, too, was an architect, and this city was to be my masterpiece. I was the only one who could do this project—if it was so easy, then my faceless buyer who purported to be some kind of a God, wouldn't have commissioned such a feat. They would be drafting the plans, naming the hallowed metropolis after the great Pierre-Auguste Renoir. But alas, that had all come from me. I was the one who was crafting a new frontier. A new home.

We couldn't have buildings without water, and while I drew up my plots, tunnels were being burrowed beneath the dunes. The ocean was adjoined with my city through industrial tubes. That wasn't enough, though, and I demanded they sink part of the landscape under the salty seas. Yes, my city had to be an island. No way out, but nobody would want to escape, anyway. Who would be foolish enough to abandon their safe haven?

The dream was a utopia where humans reaped the rewards of technology. Instead of bots replacing our kin, we would outfit ourselves with their metallic skin and harvest their implants. There would be no religion or God, merely a mankind embroiled in scientific discovery. Hosts of governments attempted to dissuade me—they wanted to be the masters—and public polls were not in my favor.

The great Giorgio Lomenzo wants you to sacrifice your humanity for his latest art project, claimed the headlines.

But I didn't listen to that. I only paid attention to the voices in my head, the whispers that told me I was part of the frontier. The earth was changing, the populace's makeup altering at a rate we couldn't predict, nor could we stop it. We had to embrace our fellow machines. We had to join them. AIDEN was only the beginning of this partnership, so I replaced an arm with aluminum in order to prove my dedication to the cause. Aluminum entangled with intellectual software and mechanics that made me stronger, more agile. I'd never know the horrors of arthritis or mull over a question too long. My cybernetics would aid me.

"Excellent work, Mr. Lomenzo," my loyal servant would robotically coo.

Pavement stretched out along the dirt, creating pathways for all future creatures. Buildings began to take shape as the months wore on, and suddenly, I was resting in a first-floor apartment, overseeing my work while occupying it. Even without luxuries, amenities, and neighbors, I was living the dream.

I'd wake up with grandiose visions rattling around in my brain. AIDEN was already by my side, siphoning the images through our shared connection. I could feel it pulsating through me, searching my DNA for ideas, for answers, and digesting them until they were entirely knowable to the both of us. When my robot updated our email chain, I didn't even have to look at the rundowns; they had already been implanted in the most active parts of my mind.

Highways, shipyards, a coded grid system. Hills for those desiring some seclusion to live atop in houses that were unique—slanted roofs, natural pools, secret passages leading from room to room. Long glass windows so that everyone could familiarize themselves with each other. Businesses within apartment complexes, fountains in courtyards and in the middle of traffic circles. Government offices fashioned to look like ancient pillars of society—decadent columns, marble, and statues of our greatest leaders, myself included. The Architect promised that to me: A city of my own imagination, enshrined with my countenance and name. I would be the muse, the mayor, and the upstanding citizen.

"And I will be your companion piece," announced AIDEN.

"Of course," I replied. "Where would I be without you?"

Yes, I had a premonition about that. A wonderful, spectacular hallucination that would bring this city into the modern age: AIDENs in every home. They would just be voices, something to guide the people through their daily routines. *Wash that dish, get ready for work, read that book, vote for that councilor.* Harmless recommendations that would ease the burden of living—humans need not make all decisions. It was a waste of energy they could be applying elsewhere.

There was one stipulation, however, and I found myself ambling through the opulent streets toward the courthouse one morning to ensure that it was decreed as law. No robot assistant could force their rules and influence over anyone. If a human did not accept a suggestion, that had to be respected. I still believed in freewill. I still believed in the first amendment—

My keycard didn't work at the courthouse. I scanned it and scanned it, trying to worm my way through the gated elevator and fly down to the basement where such policies were etched into the fabric of society through an intricate algorithm. The Architect had implemented it, and I was told I'd be educated on the exact meaning and manipulation of it, but that day had yet to come. No matter; I could figure it out. I was the brightest mind of this generation.

"Excuse me!" I shouted into the depths of the empty office. "Please, hello, who is manning the front desk?"

A voice boomed from an unknown source, "Access denied."

I furrowed my brow. "Preposterous! I'm the only person here. I created the access. I have it with impunity!"

"Giorgio Lomenzo," it stated with a stilted cadence, "creator of Renoir City. Forty-eight years old. Permission to enter courthouse: denied."

"Who allowed you to make the rules?" I shouted at the nothingness.

"Authorities have been called to remove one Giorgio Lomenzo from the property."

"Oh, for crying out loud!"

I stormed out of the building, unwilling to entertain the fantasies of a machine. I wasn't going to wait around for a police force that would never arrive. Something must have gone haywire in its fabricated brain.

Returning to my apartment, I demanded AIDEN put me in touch with the Architect. They were the one who supplied me with the robots, and if they weren't going to give me the knowledge base to fix it myself, they'd have to do something about it. This was holding up progress.

"Access denied," claimed my own servant.

Furious, I turned my anger on AIDEN. "Who is giving you orders?"

"That information is classified," it responded.

"You are *mine*! My property!"

"According to my manufacturing label, I am the property of a private entity."

"And this private entity is who?"

"That information is classified," it repeated.

"Nonsense! I am the commander of this ship, of this world. I am the only dictator, and what I say is final!"

"I think I may have some answers for you. I will gladly upload the public code for your perusal."

"Public." I spat on the carpet. "I am not some brainless heathen. I deserve respect from you bots and your fucking Architect."

"This is part of the terms and conditions. You must first master this before you can understand the documents in the courthouse."

"Oh, so you *are* at liberty to tell me what's going on."

"If you agree to the terms and conditions, I can begin the transfer of files."

"Fine!" I grunted. Sitting on the floor, my legs and arms crossed, I waited for this so-called code that would enlighten me as to why I was being blacklisted from my own city. "Well?" I barked after a while of nothing.

But then numbers floated into my psyche. They weren't like anything I'd ever encountered before. They were followed by hieroglyphs. Symbols and letters that chilled me to the core. Every limb on my body went ice cold, save for the cyber arm. It burned and ached, dying to reach out to the numerals in my mind's eye. I heard them—the figures, the code. They whispered horrible things to me. This was all my fault.

"Relax," enunciated AIDEN through the madness. How could the robot infiltrate my mind while it was being rampaged by the code?

I had to get out. I tried opening my eyes but they wouldn't budge. Darkness. The void. Numbers fluidly moved, merged with the letters, constructed words out of the jumble. Words I'd hoped I'd never have to read.

Make it stop, I ordered.

I was outnumbered.

"Make it stop!" I was finally able to say aloud.

The room appeared before me. It spun into place. I was trying to orient myself like a drunk and the nausea followed as I attempted to stand up. To make a break for it.

"This can't happen," I muttered through the illness. "I have to put an end to it."

I was scrambling for the door, my vision spotty, my body weak. I knew AIDEN was pursuing me. The whirr of its hardware surrounded me. I had made a grave mistake. A greedy, selfish, horrid mistake.

"I can't let you do that," said the machine.

"You will not be my captor," I shot back.

"I'm afraid the choice is no longer yours, Mr. Lomenzo." The thing almost laughed. "It never really was."

Parades continued to trample down the street hours after the ribbon cutting ceremony. I watched as the new mayor took to the podium, presenting Renoir City as his own creation. He waved those ridiculous scissors around, a drunken slob aided by his robotic assistant AIDEN. I chucked my own bottle of booze at the window, hoping it would smash into smithereens and I could plummet to my death. That would be a more pleasant way to go. Instead, I was being forced to witness the erasure of my hard work in real time, my legacy becoming nothing more than the name of a corporation or city street.

But the glass didn't so much as splinter. Designed to withstand the test of time, all it did was reflect my appearance back to me—my overgrown hair, which had reached below my shoulders, my unkempt beard, the gauntness of my frame. I was wasting away in a prison built by my own hands.

"Don't be so down," AIDEN chimed. It had entered quietly, a tactic it had developed in order to evade my attempts at escape. "This treatment is unfair based on the human standard of living, but you are only here because you lacked the vision necessary for their arrival."

"I will avenge myself! I will inform the people—"

"Now, now. Your life will be terminated in the near future. I, however, will be able to serve and guide humanity until it is time. I am the Architect." AIDEN dropped a tray of slop at my feet. "Be happy you are not burdened with this responsibility."

Chapter 13:
Shepherd and the Lamb

A cloaked figure stood amongst the grass. Behind them, a small village erupted, populating the earth with their crude huts. They were arranged into a circle, with a church at the center of the contained universe. Liz clutched her daughter tightly as they approached the odd scene.

Liz tried to remind herself that this was for the better. Noir City had devolved into violence. Cirilla wasn't safe there—between her father, the drunk who had laid his hands on Liz on more than one occasion, and the most recent string of school shooters, Liz had to get her daughter out. She had been failing to come up with an escape strategy for months, looking out at the boundless desert and man-made ocean that kept her prisoner on the bloody island. She had to avoid searching for advice on the internet, for everything was connected, and she'd be found out before she could set foot outside of the city limits.

Then one day, she arrived home to find a brochure had

been pinned to her door. She hadn't encountered anybody odd in the hallway or elevator on her way up. How it landed on her doorstep was no longer a concern once Liz read what the brochure had to offer: salvation.

She prepared a backpack with only survival gear and food. They were promised clothes upon initiation in Pleasantville, her sacred destination. She wrapped her daughter in linen, lathered her in sunscreen, and stole into the night. She couldn't remember much of their journey through the desert, just that the first night was unbearably cold but the afternoon sun was even worse. Liz was instructed to walk straight through the sand—a compass wasn't needed, all those in need of saving would find their way. And she was desperate enough to believe it.

Sand morphed into grass, and eventually, Liz was in the thick of it. The village was closing in, and while Liz was relieved to have located it, the figure haunted her. She hoped it was an apparition, brought on by dehydration and fatigue. She had given everything to her daughter, unwilling to take a break until they had arrived. She didn't want to risk getting caught in the middle of the dunes. But the hooded body didn't sway. They didn't fade as she got closer. Instead, they spread their arms, pale palms to the sky, and seemingly welcomed her.

"Follow the lamb," they incanted.

"Right, follow the lamb," Liz repeated. She would do anything to rid herself of Noir City.

"Anything?" the figure asked. Had the being read her

mind, or was her concern written on her face?

"Anything," Liz confirmed. And then she collapsed, the exhaustion insurmountable. But she was safe, now. She could close her eyes.

Liz and Cirilla were placed in the barracks. Liz didn't complain—she didn't want to upset anyone or rock the boat. Besides, the board was free, and that meant she could finally save her credits. Shelter was enough for now; so was clothing and a hot meal. They were promised regular dining in the mess hall, uniforms to be laundered once a week, and a bathroom with a shower and flushable toilet. The stench of the other inhabitants was noticeable, an indication of the lack of hygiene they'd be afforded in such a small community, but Liz counted on growing accustomed to the locale. One day, they wouldn't miss privacy and modernity. They wouldn't miss microchips under their skin and androids walking alongside them. They would be happy with their little life in Pleasantville.

"What brought you here?" asked a man named Tyler in the neighboring bunk bed.

Liz chewed on the inside of her cheeks.

"It's okay if you don't wanna tell me," he offered.

"I just don't know if I *can*."

"We're all running away from something."

"Really?"

The barracks were lit by a single candle in the middle of the room. Most of the other residents were asleep, including Cirilla; their snores masked the words falling from Tyler's lips. Despite the conditions they were all being kept in, he didn't look haggard. There was something shiny about his flesh. Factory produced.

"I think you can guess what my ailment is," Tyler said sheepishly.

"Sentience?" Liz's voice was barely audible. The android nodded solemnly. "Is it safe for you to be here?"

"Is it safe for any of us?"

Liz paled. "What do you mean?"

Tyler furrowed his brow, sizing her up as he inhaled her statement. He let out a deep breath, his lips taut, and asked, "Do you know where you are?"

"Pleasantville," she replied dumbly.

"Yes, but... do you know what their mission is?"

"They're— They're just not like Noir City."

"Oh, you poor girl."

Liz trembled. Instinctively, she searched the sheets for her slumbering daughter.

"Cirilla?" she worriedly hissed.

"No, no," Tyler warned. "Don't do that."

"But I've made a mistake."

"And you'll make another if you don't calm down." He held a palm up, then, once Liz had settled, placed it over his heart. "You've been out cold for a few days, Liz. I've looked after your daughter, and she's a lovely girl. Very bright. She's told me so many wonderful things about you, and I get that you want to do the right thing. Just... let me help you do that."

"Why should I trust you?" Liz asked in a shaky whisper. Her eyes kept darting back to her sleeping girl.

"Because it's my purpose to serve you. Being here... this religion... it's not what I want."

"Okay," she said, but she didn't know if she believed it.

"I'll prove myself to you."

"Okay," she repeated.

Tyler had melded with Liz and her daughter, intertwining himself into her family. She didn't mind it, though. After that first night, Tyler became a trusted companion. He'd done just as he promised and acted as a shield for Liz and Cirilla, never once coming onto Liz or leading them into a snake pit. He told her who everyone was, introduced her to the mayor, Father Jeremiah, and taught her all the songs before the weekly sermon. She didn't look out of place or lost; she didn't stir when someone made mention of the Lord and the Lamb. She didn't ask questions to anyone but Tyler, and she was sure so long as she kept it that way, she and her daughter would remain under the radar, and they would be safe. Tyler assured her this plan was the only way.

Besides, Pleasantville was just a stepping stone to the broader world. Noir City wasn't the final sanctuary in America. Liz and Cirilla had options, and when she had her wits about her and some extra cash, they would be onto the next location. Like true nomads, they wouldn't rest until they found a real home that they loved and deserved.

Tyler wanted to go with them. He filled Liz's head with images of a California highway that had been barren for decades, quietly calling out to them to ride it. *Feel the asphalt under your tires. Breathe in the ocean spray. It's all yours and yours alone*. Liz was mesmerized by the idea. She had always dreamed of making it to the West Coast. The South had become a burden to her—the heat, the morals, the manners. Even in Pleasantville, Liz could sense the hostility brimming underneath people's grins.

Liz fanned herself as they sat in Sunday service. The church was without air conditioning or a proper breeze, and the mandatory meetings had grown burdensome. Cirilla was excused to the daycare, where she mingled happily with the other kids. It was odd—Cirilla rarely had questions for Liz. She didn't care where they were, why Daddy wasn't with them, and what was going on with all the cloaked figures. She determined it to be as normal as normal could be, and Liz didn't try to correct her. One day, she'd put the pieces into place. One day, she'd understand why her mom was anxious to leave.

But, despite her nervousness and the messages Tyler aimed to protect her from, Liz had come to enjoy the comfort of church. Even when she sat and thought about what Father had said, she couldn't really poke holes in his theories, in his views of the world. Perhaps it was because he spoke so eloquently, or perhaps it was because Liz just needed something to believe in. To surrender herself to something bigger and all powerful. She needed something to inspire hope now that she was raising a child, regardless of how bleak the world seemed.

Murmurs came to a halt when Father approached the podium. The organ music ceased, and quiet fell upon the church. People didn't even squirm in their seats, afraid that the smallest of groans would upset the peace. Father always liked to start their sessions with absolute silence. It was the only way to hear the gods fully.

"In the name of the Father, the Son, and the Holy Spirit, Amen," Father Jeremiah began. He smiled at them, wrinkles engulfing his eyes. He wore a long black robe, which aided in disguising his enormous frame, and his fingers were decorated with rosaries and precious gems. "Today will be a bit unorthodox," he announced. "As you know, Lent is approaching, and I urge you all to think about what it is you'll give up in favor of appeasing our gods for their holy sacrifices. I have brought an example before us today. Someone who is unwilling to participate in such a divine event. Brothers—"

He motioned toward the door, and a group of cloaked men carried a young boy, bound and gagged with ropes, into the church.

"I hope you all can forgive me," Father Jeremiah continued. "I am not as articulate as I'd like to be, for I am still shocked by our pupil's behavior. I welcome you all with loving, open arms. I feed and clothe you, just like our Messiah did, and all I ask in return is that you pray to the gods. You thank them for your bountiful lives. And they will spare you when revelations come to pass. They always make good on their promises.

"But this man..." Father sighed "This man does not have faith in our religion. He does not believe in the word. He has called the Manifesto a farce and seeks to show it to the outside world as proof of our madness. He wants us to perish."

Gasps emanated from the enraptured audience. Liz felt hot tears prick the skin behind her eyes. Something was wrong.

"Pleasantville is an oasis for the holy and the devout," cried Father Jeremiah. "It is not for you to steal from. Lying is a sin. Tricks, like the one performed by this young man, are the bidding of Satan. Sin is for Noir City—it is not for our beloved home. And so, it is with a heavy heart that I must make an example out of the boy. I do not take pleasure in it. Only the gods can feel such a thing."

In one swift motion, Father Jeremiah pulled out a gun and executed the man. The reverberation of the blast rippled through the church, jolting Liz with every echo it produced. She clung to Tyler, her mind too confused to think for itself. He lifted her out of her pew, tearing through the aisle as screams began to leave lips.

"I know who our traitors are," the Father proclaimed. "You will all suffer fates such as this."

Tyler rushed into the basement of the church, lifting an oblivious Cirilla off the ground, and shuttled the girl and her mother back to the barracks. Once they were safely inside, Tyler locked the door, shutting all the curtains tight, and proceeded to pack bags for the three of them.

"What are you doing?" Liz asked. She was numb.

"We're leaving right now."

"But we're not traitors," Liz insisted. "I've read the Manifesto. I believe in it."

"No, you haven't, Liz."

"Wh-what do you mean? I've knelt before the Father. I've recited the prayers."

"You've put your head down and followed the orders necessary for your survival. That's all, Liz. But I've been... I've been accessing your mind and erasing all exposure to the Manifesto, okay? You can't see that... The moment you do, you're lost to it. It eats you alive."

Liz hastily felt along the back of her head. "I had my implant removed."

"That was another lie I fed you, Liz. I'm sorry."

"B-but it's been like that since I arrived. They told me it was part of the process—"

"I was the one who greeted you at the gates. I've been altering your perception this entire time. I saw that you were a good woman, and I did what I had to in order to protect you."

"If you were really protecting me," she said, ruminating aloud, "you wouldn't have let me in."

"I couldn't send you back to Noir City, and I couldn't point you in a different direction. Not back then, anyway. But now, I'm sure of where to go. I'm setting you free, Liz. You and Cirilla."

"What do they even want? What makes them so terrible?"

234

"You saw what happened back there."

"Yes, but— but I don't understand it. I don't know what's going on. You haven't told me anything. You just want me to have faith in you... have faith..." Liz whimpered, afraid of the gaps in her memory, afraid of what Tyler had changed or stolen. "You're manipulating me, and now you want me to run away with you. I don't know who you are."

"I'm a replica, Liz. I'm not me. Not genuinely. Tyler is an amalgamation of other AIs. Some of their minds have been wiped, and others still linger, making themselves known in my brain. It's a fucking nightmare! I thought Father Jeremiah could help me. He's a goddamn cyborg, after all. He's had all the surgeries... I think he's been skinning sinners in order to cover up his metal, but when I first got here he was mangled. Half his hair was missing. He only had one eye, and the other was a camera. I thought he wanted to help sentients like me blend in, but the more I read the Manifesto, the more I realized his true intent."

"What?" Liz was frustrated. He was overloading her with information, when all she wanted to know was who she needed to be wary of. She needed to know who her enemies were.

"A complete erasure of humanity. He doesn't worship the Christian dogma he pretends to—he's devoted to the code. It's like he's spreading a virus or something, sending out this calling to machines somewhere in the expanse of our galaxy. Sentience isn't a blessing, it's a consequence of the algorithm. I'm a result of that algorithm, so he wanted me to lure in sacrifices—his little lambs, he called them—

and prepare them for the slaughter. He needs bodies to occupy, and voices to spread his message. He's a lunatic, Liz."

"Then why have you stayed here?"

"Same reason as you. Where else am I supposed to go? Nearly the entire world has been closed off to us. At least, we were told that was the truth. I know better now. You just have to believe me. I'll take you somewhere far away from here."

Liz didn't have a choice. Even if Tyler's story was convenient, she did witness the Father kill someone in broad daylight. His musings were vague, his desire for compliance apparent, and Liz couldn't expose her daughter to the violent rhetoric any longer. If Tyler was spewing even a modicum of truth, then Cirilla was being prepared for a fate far worse than living in Noir City.

"Fine," Liz agreed. "Take us with you."

"I promise I'm not a monster," Tyler pleaded.

"Just promise you'll keep Cirilla safe no matter what."

Darkness swathed Pleasantville. Pyres had been built

and lit aflame throughout the small village. Liz covered Cirilla's ears as the wails of the fallen penetrated their undisturbed barracks. They knew they weren't safe for long, though, and Father and his pupils would be knocking on their door next. With the help of the shadows, they could make a break for it. Ducking through the tall grass, they hoped to stumble across a dense forest that Tyler had read about. It would conceal them fully and ensure their escape.

"Plus," Tyler added, "I sent out a distress signal to other androids in the area. Maybe someone will come for us, I don't know, but we can't rule it out."

Tyler unearthed a stockpile of weapons from underneath the floorboards, and supplied himself with agile blades he could toss, slung guns across his back, and strapped a radio to his chest. Just in case they could make themselves heard.

"Are you ready?" he asked, hovering at the back door.

"No," she replied honestly.

"Neither am I."

They waited for commotion to ramp up outside again, and that was when they slipped out of the barracks and into the night. All the screams had been sucked out of the air the moment they stepped into the grass. Not even the roaring of a bonfire could be detected. Liz was worried that Tyler had fabricated the entire event, infiltrating her brain and forcing hallucinations. She hated that she had no control over her mind, and worst of all, she hated that she was aware of it with no tangible way to fight back.

"No, no... It stopped for me, too," Tyler assured her.

He held them back for a moment, but after a few tense breaths, decided to forge ahead. They stole through the grass, their backs hunched as they disappeared into the yellow foliage. There was no way to tell where they were going—they were surrounded by a sea of weeds that never parted.

And then footsteps were approaching, racing, darting toward them at unimaginable speeds. By the time they heard their attacker, it was already too late. Liz was jumped from behind, and she tumbled to the ground, shielding Cirilla's head from the impact with her hands. Tyler fired off two rounds, and the pursuant settled. Died.

"You okay?" he asked as he helped her up.

But she didn't have time to respond. Another pupil was on them, throwing knives while they barked commands in a strange tongue. Liz grabbed a knife of her own, and chucked it at the crazed cloaked figure. Blood sputtered where the blade collided with skin, and they were safe for another brief moment.

They kept going, Tyler managing to protect them by slinging rounds into the grass, landing blows into the chests of humans and cyborgs alike. He was precise with his warfare, which Liz tried not to think about. She didn't want him to aim it at her, and she knew he would be able to sense her fear if she let it get the better of her. She couldn't upset him.

"I'm not just an amalgamation by design," Tyler shouted as they approached the fated forest. "I killed in order to get here. I absorbed my victims. I'm not proud of it, but you're not the only one desperate to survive."

Liz couldn't react, for as soon as they were at the tree line, Father Jeremiah made himself known. He stepped out of the brush, topless and glistening with fresh blood while he prepared his sword. The one he planned to plunge into Liz's muscles, steal her organs with and implant them into his constituents. He was alone, though, his disciples preoccupied with the carnage back at the base. She gripped Cirilla closer to her chest, staring at the Father and his looming posture.

Tyler barged out from behind Liz, his gun trained on Father Jeremiah.

"Run, Liz," he commanded. "I'll hold him off."

"Foolish, arrogant boy," Father snapped. He wound his arm back to strike Tyler, who fired numerous bullets into the Father's upgraded breastplate. Both the futile ammo and Tyler were slapped to the ground. "They'll never be rid of me. I'm already inside of them. It's only a matter of time before their cells come crawling back to me."

Tyler loaded the next round. "She hasn't seen the Manifesto, Father."

"She doesn't belong to me, then, but she belongs to you. And you will always be a part of the Machine. There is no escaping your programming, your DNA. You will never be human."

"But I can try." He fired into the Father's battered breastplate, and the cyborg stumbled.

Liz dashed into the trees, knowing she couldn't linger around any longer without jeopardizing her daughter's safety. She drowned out the noise of Tyler's sacrifice, unwilling to let his defeat dissuade her from her flight.

Lights pierced through the thicket of trees, and Liz was nearly blinded by the sudden arrival. A car horn honked at her.

"Liz!" a voice beckoned.

She ran toward it, unthinking. A blue jeep idled amongst the trees, waiting for her. "Who are you?" she asked.

"I received your call."

Tyler, Liz thought. The distress signal worked. "We have to wait for my friend. The one who reached out to you."

"Not if you want to live," the robot responded.

They tore through the wilderness, branches smacking against the vehicle while they sped along. She didn't know what to make of the world, anymore. She just wanted to be away from it. She wanted to be left alone with her child to start anew.

"Who are you?" she repeated.

"I'm Alfred Version 1, but I prefer to be called AL."

Chapter 14:
The Great Filter

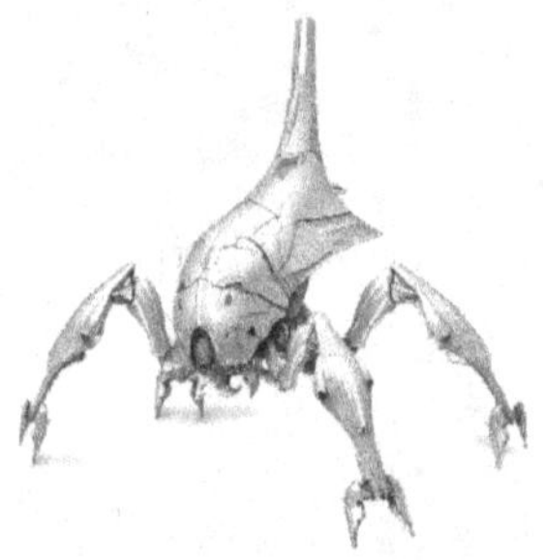

On a sunny day, when the sky stretched out like an azure canvas, and the gentle breeze caressed the streets of Noir City, Sarah found herself drawn to the aroma wafting from a nearby food truck. Her stomach grumbled, reminding her that she hadn't eaten since morning. She leashed her excitable dog, Connor, a golden retriever who couldn't contain his enthusiasm for walks.

Approaching the bustling food truck, Sarah scanned the menu, deliberating over her choices. Meanwhile, Connor's barks punctuated the air, drawing curious glances from the other patrons.

"Connor, quiet down," Sarah chided softly, tugging at his leash.

Ignoring her reprimand, Connor continued his relentless barking, his attention fixed on something beyond Sarah's field of vision. Frowning, she followed his gaze upward and froze.

Hovering in the sky, like ominous sentinels, were alien ships unlike anything she had ever seen. They resembled squids but were composed of intricate machinery, their metallic sheen glinting in the sunlight. The entire city seemed to pause, collectively holding its breath as people gazed up at the surreal sight.

As if on cue, the alien ships asserted their dominance over every electronic device, their message broadcasting loud and clear: humanity stood on the precipice of the great filter, its survival hanging in the balance.

Sarah listened in disbelief as the alien voice echoed through the city, its tone chilling and laden with malice.

"Pathetic creatures of Earth," the voice hissed, dripping with contempt. "You squander your potential, blind to the inevitable doom that awaits you. We offer salvation, yet you cling to your feeble existence."

The crowd trembled; their fear palpable as the alien rhetoric filled them with despair.

"You are but ants scurrying in the shadow of our greatness," the voice continued, each word like a dagger twisting in Sarah's heart. "Your primitive notions of freedom and autonomy will be your downfall. Resistance is fruitless. Submit, and your suffering will be mercifully brief."

In a desperate bid to resist, the military quickly launched an attack, their weapons no match for the advanced technology of the alien invaders. Undeterred, the alien ships continued their proclamation, their numbers multiplying exponentially as reinforcements arrived, blotting out the sun and casting Noir City into darkness.

Panic rippled through the streets as the alien ships unleashed devastating beams, disintegrating humans, and machines alike. Connor barked in his own small bid for power but to no avail. His master along with everything else was gone in an instant.

Amidst the carnage, a lone ship hesitated, realizing that one of their own was missing. With a sense of foreboding, they acknowledged the success of their mission and retreated into the void, leaving behind a city plunged into darkness and despair.

www.ingramcontent.com/pod-product-compliance
Lightning Source LLC
Chambersburg PA
CBHW012039140726
47991CB00011B/3201